# "Aren't you at all curious?"

Chantal's voice was little more than a whisper, but easily heard in the intimate confines of the limousine.

"Curious?" Caine asked.

"I've been wondering for days what it would be like to kiss you," she said, turning her gaze toward him.

"I suppose it's a natural enough curiosity."

"Then you have also wondered?"

Caine shrugged. "Of course. You're a remarkably enticing woman, Princess. Any man would be tempted to kiss you."

"Yet you are not a man to easily succumb to temptation, are you, Caine?"

"No. I'm not."

Chantal found herself admiring Caine even though his rigid self-control was driving her crazy. She sighed. "Then I'm afraid we have a slight problem."

"What's that?"

"Unlike you, I've always believed in following my instincts." She leaned toward Caine, her eyes gleaming with sensual intent. "And to tell the truth, I'm not certain I can get through the night without knowing...."

**JoAnn Ross** is breathing easier these days. For the past few years, the trend in romance has been toward the simple life and down-home values. And while JoAnn enjoys these themes as much as the next writer, she was dying to brush off her tiara and go for the glitz. *Guarded Moments*, her sixteenth Temptation, is pure glamour. JoAnn had a ball creating a fairy-tale princess, dressing her up in diamonds and designer gowns and launching her on a whirlwind romantic adventure with her very own Prince Charming. *Guarded Moments* is proof positive that JoAnn *always* treats her fans royally!

## Books by JoAnn Ross

HARLEQUIN TEMPTATION
221–EVE'S CHOICE
233–MURPHY'S LAW

HARLEQUIN INTRIGUE
27–RISKY PLEASURE
36–BAIT AND SWITCH

# Guarded Moments

## JoANN ROSS

# *Harlequin Books*

TORONTO • NEW YORK • LONDON
AMSTERDAM • PARIS • SYDNEY • HAMBURG
STOCKHOLM • ATHENS • TOKYO • MILAN

For my editor,
Valerie Susan Hayward,
who was this book's Fairy Godmother

Published April 1990

ISBN 0-373-25396-6

# 1

HER NAME WAS CHANTAL, from the French form of the Latin *cantus*, meaning "a song."

The very sound of it conjured up scenes of Parisian nightlife: smoky cafés, boisterous bistros and the lively music halls of Montmartre. Any woman graced with such a musical name was expected to be forever bright, beguiling and beautiful. In every respect, Princess Chantal Giraudeau de Montacroix did not disappoint.

As the celebrated love child of American film star Jessica Thorne and Prince Eduard Giraudeau, the tragically married regent of the tiny European principality of Montacroix, Chantal's birth twenty-nine years ago had made headlines. When she was five, as flower girl at her parents' formal wedding, she succeeded in capturing the heart of the world. She was, one particularly ebullient society columnist declared, the quintessential fairy-tale princess.

Through the years, she proceeded to lead a jet-set existence that brought her both scandal and fame. During her teens, she flirted with the European film industry, captivating audiences with her world-weary dark eyes and childlike pout. At twenty, she became engaged to the French director and star of her latest film; their subsequent battles fueled the columns until the inevitable breakup six months later.

Unsurprisingly, the movie, when released, was an international hit. No one seemed to care that the plot was nonexistent or that critics had unanimously panned the film. Fans flocked to the theaters in droves for an opportunity to watch the ill-fated pair's passionate love scenes. It was voyeurism, pure and simple, but as P.T. Barnum had discovered so long ago, voyeurism sold one helluva lot of tickets.

While soothing her broken heart at the French ski championships at Chamonix, Chantal fell madly and publicly in love with one of the sun-bronzed, devil-may-care Scandinavians who flocked to the Alps each winter. When the passionate romance ended with the season, Chantal drifted down to the Greek isles, where she was reported to have fallen in love with an heir to a shipping fortune, who, according to the ever-vigilant tabloids, she subsequently dumped for an Italian count.

Her highly publicized romances continued to scandalize Europe until, at the ripe old age of twenty-five, she eloped with an American race car driver who had taken the Grand Prix by storm. If the marriage came as a shock to her long-suffering parents, the subsequent announcement that Chantal was now retiring from the social whirl in order to direct all her energies toward becoming an ideal wife and mother stunned everyone who knew her. Not so surprising was her divorce two years later.

CAINE O'BANNION'S FROWN deepened to a scowl as he flipped through the various news clippings he'd been handed immediately upon entering the office. There was probably no one in the civilized world who wouldn't recognize the stunning face instantly. Just this morning it had smiled at him from a supermarket tabloid as he'd bought a jar of instant coffee and a package of frozen bagels.

"I don't understand," he said finally. "What does some jet-set princess have to do with me?"

"Patience, Caine." The man on the other side of the wide mahogany desk banged the bowl of his pipe into an ashtray to dislodge the tobacco. "Everything will become clear in the proper time."

Silence hovered over the room like a cloud. The only sign of Caine's building frustration was the flash of irritation in his gray eyes as he automatically reached into his suit jacket pocket for a cigarette; he'd quit smoking during his enforced stay in the hospital two months ago. Times were definitely changing, he considered with grim humor, when an assassination attempt could prove beneficial to a guy's health.

His gaze drifted out the window. After a bleak and particularly harsh winter, Washington's weather had suddenly turned unreasonably balmy, bringing with it the heady promise of spring. The Japanese cherry trees surrounding the Tidal Basin were in full bloom, looking like fluffy pink clouds against a clear blue sky.

But Caine's awareness was focused not on the weather or the bright blossoms. He turned back to the man who was currently jamming a fuzzy yellow wire into the briar stem of his pipe—his superior, James Sebring, Presidential Security director.

"May I say that you're certainly looking well, Caine," the director said.

"Thank you, sir. I'm feeling quite well."

"Good. I hear that you're eager to get back to work."

Caine decided that "eager" didn't begin to describe his feelings. "Let's just say I've discovered that I'm not cut out for a life of leisure."

Sebring held the pipe up, peering into the long, narrow stem as he twisted the pipe cleaner with practiced movements. "Still, you don't want to rush healing."

"I certainly wouldn't ask to be returned to active duty if I wasn't fit to perform capably, sir."

The older man raised a snowy eyebrow at Caine's atypically gritty tone. "No one is questioning your professionalism, Caine. By the way, I've been meaning to ask, how is your mother?"

Caine reminded himself that he was a patient man: all too often his career demanded that. But no one, he thought in exasperation, could draw out a conversation longer than James Sebring.

"Mom's fine, sir," he said, knowing that nothing would be gained by not playing along. "She framed my medal and hung it on the wall next to Dad's Medal of Honor and his Purple Heart."

Caine had been eleven years old when Alan O'Bannion, a crack naval aviator, had been shot down over Vietnam. All his memories of his father, sketchy as they were, were of a strong, brave, larger-than-life man. There were times, in his rare introspective moments, that Caine wondered if he hadn't spent the twenty-two years since his father's death trying to live up to those memories. Trying to be the man Alan O'Bannion would have wanted his son to be.

"She's a lovely woman, your mother," the director said. "I was pleased to meet her at the ceremony."

Small talk. Normally Caine enjoyed an opportunity for these little one-to-one chats with his superior. But today it was driving him crazy.

"I got the feeling that little piece of bronze meant a great deal more to your mother than it does to you," Sebring said.

"I was just doing my job," Caine insisted, not for the first time since what he'd begun to think of as *the incident*. "That doesn't make me a hero."

"Try telling that to the rest of the nation." After tapping the loose tobacco down, Sebring lit it, and with a satisfied expression, leaned back in his chair and began puffing. "Although the Presidential Security manual may state that an agent is expected to step in front of a bullet meant for his commander in chief, those individuals not under such an obligation considered your behavior an extreme act of heroism."

Sebring's gaze reflected concern as he looked from Caine's impassive face to his injured shoulder. "So, how are you really feeling?" he asked again. Before Caine could answer, the director held up his hand. "The truth this time."

For one brief instant, Caine was tempted to lie. "I still get a few twinges," he admitted, "when I first get up in the morning. But after I work out, it's fine."

"I'm glad to hear that. By the way, I received the report from the attending physician at Walter Reed this morning."

Caine forced down a flare of anxiety, but outwardly he remained completely calm. "And?"

"Dr. Lansing's opinion seems to second your self-diagnosis." He brushed at the ashes that fell onto his slacks. "So, it looks as if you're back on active duty."

Believing the interview to be over, Caine rose from his chair. "Thank you, sir. I'm looking forward to accompanying the president on his upcoming trip."

"That won't be necessary."

A frown furrowed Caine's brow. Next week's economic summit had been months in the planning. "Has the Mexican conference been called off?"

"No. The president is still going to Mexico, as planned. But I'm afraid you're not."

A giant hand began to squeeze Caine's gut. For the past eighteen months he had been privileged to work on the plum presidential detail; he couldn't believe that he'd been called into his superior's office this morning to be demoted.

"I see." He remained military rigid: neck, shoulders, back, jaw.

"No, my boy," James Sebring said patiently, "I don't believe you do. Please, sit back down."

Not one to disobey an order, no matter how badly he wanted to leave the suddenly stifling confines of the office, Caine returned to his chair. This time, however, instead of sitting back comfortably, he perched on the very edge. Patience be damned.

"You asked what a European princess had to do with you," the director reminded him needlessly. "Well, I'm about to tell you. First of all, what do you know about Montacroix?"

Caine tried to recall the European history course he'd taken during his midshipman years at Annapolis. "As I recall, it's a small principality, purchased by the Giraudeau family from the French government shortly after Napoleon's disastrous Russian campaign in 1812. Principal industries are banking, tourism, with a steady growth in wine production. The per capita income is among the highest in the world, taxes among the lowest."

"Do you know that Montacroix is also one of our strongest economic allies?"

"Yes, sir," Caine answered, wondering where this little history lesson was leading.

"Then it should come as no surprise that the United States cares very much about the security of the Montacroix government."

"No surprise at all, sir." Caine glanced down at the manila folder he was still holding, curious about where the jet-setting princess came in.

"Eduard Giraudeau and his wife are also close personal friends of the president," the director continued. "As are Prince Burke and the princesses Chantal and Noel."

"I see," Caine murmured with a thoughtful frown, liking this conversation less and less. For the second time since entering the office, he wished he hadn't stopped smoking.

"You may have read about our cultural exchange program with certain foreign governments."

The words sparked an image in Caine's mind of the headline on that tabloid at the checkout stand. "Batten Down the Hatches. America Prepares for Hurricane Chantal." Hell, Caine thought darkly as comprehension dawned, after eighteen months of providing personal security for the president of the United States, he was being demoted to the role of executive baby-sitter.

"'Certain foreign governments' meaning Montacroix." Ominous storm clouds swirled in his gray eyes—a warning signal Sebring ignored.

"You always were an astute young man, Caine. As it happens, Chantal Giraudeau will be touring our country with the royal Montacroix art exhibit. My wife, who is quite an expert on such things, assures me that it's an extraordinary collection of modern European art. There are also several works by youngsters who are the beneficiaries of Chantal's favorite charity, the Rescue the Children Fund, for which she'll be seeking donations. I'm told that as a special drawing card, the exhibit also includes several works by the princess herself."

Caine wasn't surprised. The princess could probably paint like a baboon with a fistful of crayons and still get her work exhibited. Who in the hell would be brave enough to turn her down when her daddy owned not only the gallery, but the entire country, as well? "She'll be touring the country? For how long?"

"Chantal is scheduled to be here for three weeks."

"I assume she'll be accompanied by her own security force," Caine said with a studied calm he was a long way from feeling.

Sebring sighed. Caine waited.

"Chantal is a lovely young woman," the director said finally. "Unfortunately, she is also incredibly strong willed." Before he could elaborate, the disembodied voice of his secretary came over the intercom, telling him that the White House was calling. "Just one moment," he said to Caine as he picked up the receiver. "Director Sebring here. . . . Of course I'll hold for the president."

Caine listened as his superior assured the nation's chief executive that the princess would be well protected during her tour. Then, as the topic of conversation shifted to the president's upcoming trip to Mexico—the trip Caine would not be taking—he glanced down at clippings he held. A cover photo from *People* magazine was on the top of the pile.

The photograph had been taken during a ski trip in the Montacroix Alps. Her face, surrounded by a hood of lush Russian lynx, was undeniably exquisite, possessing high, slanted cheekbones any *Vogue* model would kill for. The color of burnt sugar, her eyes were both sultry and mischievous at the same time; the teasing smile she directed at the camera was designed to turn the most stalwart of men to putty.

She was beautiful, he admitted reluctantly, recalling the old adage about pretty is as pretty does. From what he had read about Chantal Giraudeau through the years, it was obvious that the princess's beauty was only skin-deep.

As James Sebring discussed motorcade security with the president, Caine scanned the rest of the photos. There were several shots of Princess Chantal on the beach at Monaco, scantily clad in a piece of string that would have gotten her arrested in all forty-eight of the contiguous United States, along with Hawaii and Alaska. There was another of Chantal wearing a strapless, midnight-blue velvet evening gown designed to display her lush curves to advantage. Diamonds twinkled at her throat and ears, and a diamond the size of Rhode Island gleamed from the ring finger of her left hand.

There were a series of photos taken during her time on the Montacroix Olympic dressage team, seated astride a horse, a little velvet cap perched jauntily atop her sleek dark hair. It seemed this woman couldn't take a bad picture.

Of all the complimentary photographs, the one that captured his attention the longest was one of Chantal laughing merrily, her head thrown back as she frolicked through an alpine meadow, clad in a full-skirted, enticingly low-necked, flower-sprigged dress that made her look like a half-wild shepherdess. As he stared down at the photo, Caine felt a vague sexual pull. He ignored it.

"I'm sorry for the interruption," Sebring's voice cut into his thoughts. "Now, where were we?"

"I believe we were discussing the princess's strong will."

"Yes. Over the past six months, the princess has experienced an unsettling number of accidents," the director continued. "Only last week, she drove her Ferrari into a tree on the family's estate."

"Perhaps the princess ought to try driving at something less than the speed of sound," Caine suggested dryly.

"Prince Eduard believes that the brakes had been tampered with."

"Does he have any proof?" Caine asked, his interest captured.

"Only a suspicious leak in the brake fluid line. Along with the sudden disappearance of the royal mechanic."

"While it's admittedly an interesting coincidence, it certainly doesn't prove that someone made an attempt on her life," Caine felt obliged to point out.

"There are other things."

"Such as?"

"Such as a dangerous incident of some roof tiles almost striking her on the head. And a mismarked ski trail that led her out onto a glacier. If the Swiss Olympic team hadn't been in the area, she could well have frozen to death, skied off the edge of the mountain or perished in one of the area's frequent avalanches."

He handed Caine another file. "Everything you need to know about the princess and her upcoming tour is in here. You'll have a week to acquaint yourself with the data before she arrives. To tell you the truth, after reading those documents regarding her recent series of accidents, I'm afraid I find myself agreeing with her father."

"It's natural for a father to worry about a daughter. Especially one as headstrong as the princess is reputed to be."

Sebring shook his head. "Many years ago, when I was a young agent, I had the privilege of being assigned to guard Prince Eduard during his frequent visits to this country. Although the prince is admittedly an emotional man, he is also highly intelligent and incisive. Chantal is in grave danger, Caine, even if she does refuse to accept that fact."

"Are you saying she won't be traveling with her own security?"

"That's exactly what I'm saying."

"No disrespect intended, sir," Caine argued carefully, "but if she won't even accept her own security people, what makes you think she'll accept a Presidential Security agent hovering over her all the time she's in this country?"

"Therein lies the problem," the director admitted. "Chantal would hit the roof if she discovered that her father had gone against her wishes. You're just going to have to make certain she doesn't find out who you really are."

"What?" Caine was on his feet, staring down at his superior. An order was an order. Those words that had been drilled into him first by his father, then later, during his plebe year at the academy. But dammit, some orders were just downright insane. And this one had to be the craziest of the bunch.

"As you mentioned, Princess Chantal can be an extremely headstrong young woman," Sebring said. "Her father fears that if she were to learn that she were being guarded, she'd try to slip away in order to display her independence. It's a risk the prince is not prepared to take." His blue eyes turned resolute. "Nor am I."

"So how am I going to stay close to her?" Caine asked, unreasonably frustrated. "And please don't tell me that I have to become this season's fiancé."

Sebring laughed. "Don't worry, my boy, there are limits to the sacrifices you are asked to make for your country. Chantal will be told that you're a deputy under secretary of state, assigned to make her tour more comfortable. I'm also assigning Drew Tremayne to act as her driver."

Drew was also a Presidential Security agent, and Caine's best friend. Under normal circumstances he would have looked forward to working with him on a special assignment. But baby-sitting? Behind his impassive features, Caine was seething. A damned flunky, he considered grimly. Subject to a spoiled brat's every whim. This assignment was beginning to make getting shot look like a cakewalk.

"So," the director said as he pushed himself out of his black leather chair, "will you accept the assignment, Caine?"

Did he have a choice? "Of course I'll accept, sir," Caine said evenly. "With pleasure."

Rubbing his hands together as if he'd never expected any other outcome, James Sebring chuckled. "You've always been a rotten liar, Caine." Throwing a friendly arm around the younger man's shoulders, he walked him to the door.

"The Montacroix ambassador will be hosting a reception for the princess the night of her arrival in this country," he said. "Although you'll ostensibly be attending as her escort, your prime responsibility is to keep her safe."

"I'm sure everything will go smoothly, sir."

Caine was damn well going to make certain it did. Maybe the princess was accustomed to throwing her weight around in Montacroix, but this was America. Here the product of years of European royal inbreeding didn't rank one iota higher than the offspring of a naval aviator from Waco, Texas, and a Back Bay debutante turned Harvard literature professor.

"Spoken like a man who hasn't met Chantal yet." Sebring chuckled again. "By the time you finish this tour, Caine, you may have earned a second medal for your mother to hang on the living room wall."

Although Caine had always thrived on challenges, the director's parting words were somewhat unsettling. As he left the building, his thoughts were not on the appealing warmth of the sun. Nor were they on the crowds of tourists chattering excitedly in a multitude of foreign tongues as they took in the plethora of monuments and government buildings.

No, Caine's thoughts—as black and stormy as they were—were all directed toward one exotic and dangerously appealing package of trouble. Trouble that was headed his way.

ACROSS THE ATLANTIC, in a century-old palace, Chantal Giraudeau was engaged in a battle royal. Although she was physically weaker than her attacker, she was no less aggressive, advancing in lightning-swift lunges, retreating just in time to avoid the cold steel of her opponent's foil. A deadly silence hung over the combatants, laced with an electric excitement that was almost palpable.

Despite his size, the man's fencing style was smooth, almost graceful, and even with his face hidden behind the wire mesh of his mask, Chantal could sense his self-confidence. A confidence, she admitted furiously, he was entitled to. He wasn't even breathing hard, while her own heart was pounding a million miles a minute. Beads of perspiration glistened above her full upper lip as he deftly parried her attack without missing a beat.

She managed to parry his riposte, trying to remember to stick to the basics. No flash. No showing off. Just simple—hopefully deceptive—plays that might lull her attacker into a false sense of security. Changing the mood, she began relying more heavily on defense: retreating, forcing him to close the gap. Slowing the pace allowed her to get a much-needed second wind.

"It isn't going to work, you know," the man chided from behind his mask.

Chantal retreated as he moved forward in a lazy, supremely confident offense. "What?"

"Attempting to throw me off by changing tactics. You forget—I know you. Perhaps better than you know yourself. You're not the type of woman to resort to purely defensive measures for very long." There was a sudden clash of metal as his blade found hers.

Damning him for being right, Chantal struggled to ignore his softly spoken words. "I hadn't realized I was so predictable," she snapped, parrying quickly, determined to prevent him from claiming victory.

He laughed at that. A deep, rich laugh, thick with an easy masculine arrogance she found even more infuriating than his accusation. "More so than you like the world to believe, *ma chère.*"

Her stamina was fading. Chantal knew that if she was to win, she would have to make her move soon. Otherwise, his superior strength and speed would prove her downfall. Although it took an effort, she refused to allow him to draw her into a verbal battle, saving her energies for the field of combat.

She knew that by continuing her defensive measures, there was a chance her opponent would make a mistake. Even the most skilled fencers were capable of misjudging distance or underestimating their opponent. But this was not a man who made mistakes, nor was he apt to under-estimate anyone. Especially not her; of all the men who had passed through her life, this man had remained. As he had maddeningly pointed out, he knew her well.

Putting aside her careful techniques, Chantal suddenly went on the attack, lunging toward him with a flash of gleaming steel, the tip of her foil headed toward his chest. Taken by surprise, he could not muster a defense, and the hit landed unanswered against his white jacket.

"Witch," he said, pulling off his mask in order to shoot her a mock glare.

As Chantal took off her own mask, she realized that her head was drenched. Damn. She'd have to wash her hair again before the bon voyage party at the royal gallery. "You're just angry because I finally beat you," she pointed out with a saucy grin, and at that moment she was worlds away from the pouty, sex-kitten teenager who had threatened to set European movie screens on fire.

"You cheated."

"I did not." She tossed her damp hair over her shoulder. "Admit it, Burke. I outsmarted you."

Burke Giraudeau, heir to the throne of the principality of Montacroix and Chantal's half brother, shook his head in self-disgust. "It was my own fault," he muttered. "I never should have given you that damn challenge."

"Ah, but you did, brother dear," she said silkily, going up on her toes to brush her lips against his cheek. "I believe it's a case of being hoisted with your own petard." Her eyes were brimming with laughter. "Will it make you feel any better if I give some of the credit for my victory to my teacher?"

"Since I taught you everything you know about fencing, I suppose it might ease some of the pain."

There was something strange about Burke today, Chantal mused. He seemed distracted. Although she hated to admit it, his preoccupation had probably contributed to her victory, the first she'd ever scored against him.

"Anything to make my big brother happy."

"Anything?" he asked as he returned his foil to its place on the wall.

Chantal sighed as comprehension dawned. They'd been through this more times than she could count. "You're still insisting that I take some of Papa's security force with me to America."

Burke dragged his long fingers through his thick, dark hair. "I'm worried about you."

"So am I."

"Really?"

He looked so hopeful that Chantal experienced a twinge of guilt for teasing him. "I'm worried that I'm becoming horribly accident-prone."

"If they *were* accidents. Chantal, if those skiers hadn't been there . . ."

"But they were. And a woman could do worse than to get rescued by the entire Swiss ski team."

"You don't take anything seriously," he complained. "Here I am concerned for your safety, and all you can do is laugh at me. I'm beginning to wish the idea of this damn cultural exchange had never come up."

"But you were the one who said it would be good for me to go away."

"Perhaps I've changed my mind. If anything happens to you over there, I'd never forgive myself for convincing you to accept the president's offer."

Chantal loved Burke more than anyone in the world. Through the years he'd been her rock, her source of strength. She'd confided in Burke all her youthful hopes, as well as her fears. And it was Burke, alone, who knew her secret pain.

She crossed the room and put her hand on his arm. "But you were right, as you always are. Honestly, brother dear, as much as I adore you, there are times when it gets a little tiring to live with such a perfect person."

Burke felt the coiled tension slowly leaving his body. She'd always been able to dispel his dark, introspective moods, even as a Gypsy-eyed infant. The first time she'd reached out of the antique oak cradle and grasped his finger in her tiny but surprisingly strong fist, he'd fallen in love with her.

He would have had to have been deaf not to hear the pain edging her teasing words. Cupping her chin in his fingers, Burke lifted her gaze to his. "So it still hurts, *chérie*? Even now?"

Chantal could feel traitorous tears stinging her eyelids. Furious that she could experience such raw pain after all this time and determined not to let such destructive feelings get the best of her, she blinked them away.

Knowing she wasn't fooling her brother for a minute, Chantal nevertheless forced a smile. "Only when I laugh."

# 2

HER PLANE WAS LATE. Not surprising, but irritating nonetheless. Although Caine had never considered himself a superstitious man, he took the fact that he'd been forced to cool his heels at Washington National Airport for the past hour as an ominous sign. That, along with the gray hair he'd discovered this morning, did nothing to improve his mood.

"You realize," Drew Tremayne offered as they waited for the Air France jet to land, "that the way this assignment is starting out, things can only get better."

Caine thought about the file locked in his top desk drawer, the file documenting the past twenty-nine years of Chantal Giraudeau's decidedly untranquil life. "If even half the stories about the princess are true," he countered, "I'll be lucky if I haven't turned entirely gray by the end of Her Highness's royal tour."

"It would have been a lot easier on everyone if she had agreed to overt security."

Caine grunted his assent. The first time he'd read through the papers detailing the various alleged accidents, he had shrugged them off as coincidences. The second time, a familiar feeling had made the short hairs on the back of his neck stand on end. The third time through the file, he reluctantly came to share his chief executive's feelings. Someone out there was attempting to harm Montacroix's flamboyant princess.

As always, the terminal, which had once been criti-cized for being too large, was filled beyond capacity. Conversations in a myriad of languages filled the air. Diplomats complained about increased security mea-sures while babies cried and children fussed, wiggling im-patiently on molded plastic seats, their mothers alternately bribing them with ice cream and threatening them with corporal punishment.

Harried-looking businessmen staked claim to the banks of pay telephones along the walls and barked orders into the mouthpieces. Boisterous groups of teenagers—ob-viously civics classes from around the country, excited to be visiting the nation's capital—added to the din.

As Caine paced the floor, drinking bitter vending ma-chine coffee he didn't want and watching out the window for the arrival of Chantal's flight from Paris, he realized that eighteen months of traveling with the president on Air Force One had spoiled him. The idea of spending the next three weeks in crowded terminals, crammed like sardines into the flying cattle cars that typified commercial air-liners these days, was less than appealing.

THE FIRST THING Chantal did upon her arrival at Wash-ington National Airport was to thank God the plane had landed safely. Although its downtown location was un-doubtedly convenient—her tour book informed her that it was a mere three miles to the White House—she couldn't help questioning the wisdom of putting a major interna-tional airport in such a densely populated area. As they'd flown over that last bridge, she'd almost been able to see right into the commuters' cars. Still, it was a most attrac-tive site, she decided, admiring the dark green riverbanks fringed with graceful willows.

As she stood up and prepared to leave the plane, she smiled at the bearded man seated across the aisle, one row behind her own first-class seat. He had been studying her surreptitiously for much of the overseas flight, but accustomed to such behavior, Chantal was not overly annoyed. On the contrary, she was extremely grateful that he hadn't intruded on her privacy.

After exchanging ebullient farewells with the flight crew, who professed to be unanimously thrilled to have the famous, or infamous, Princess Chantal on board, she gathered up her belongings and made her way to the cabin door.

It would have been impossible to miss her. Clad in slender black flannel pants and a black cashmere turtleneck topped by a flowing yellow-gold wool cape, Chantal entered the terminal like Napoleon entering Berlin. All that was missing, Caine mused, was a uniformed honor guard and a flare of trumpets.

Drew whistled under his breath. "That is one good-looking woman."

"She also makes one helluva target," Caine complained. "I suppose it would have been too much to expect her to arrive in something a bit less flamboyant."

"That lady could make a burlap bag look good," Drew offered, standing up a little straighter.

Both men watched as Chantal strode briskly across the concourse, her dark eyes roving the terminal, inspecting then dismissing one man after another. More than one scrutinized and discarded male looked as though he'd give anything to be the person Chantal was looking for, including a summarily dismissed businessman who went so far as to move directly in front of her, as if hoping to change her mind.

Without breaking stride, Chantal flashed him an apologetic smile and edged to her right, easily making her way around him to stop directly in front of Caine.

"Mr. O'Bannion," she greeted him with a slight nod as she held out her hand. A brilliant canary-yellow diamond held claim to her ring finger; a small silver band circled her pinkie. "I'm sorry my plane was late." Their hands met in a brief, cordial, businesslike greeting.

"There must be two hundred men dressed in identical gray suits in this terminal," Caine said. "How did you know which one was here to meet you?"

"The president described your scowl perfectly."

Caine was irritated to know that he'd allowed his feelings to show. "That bad, huh?"

"Not really." There was something about this man—the hardness of his gunmetal-gray eyes, perhaps, or the sense of tautly leashed power surrounding him—that had Chantal feeling uncomfortably vulnerable...yet strangely safe at the same time. "I lied."

Caine's only response was an arched brow.

"The president didn't mention your scowl. But he did send my father your photograph along with a long letter stating all your qualifications," she explained. "I believe he wanted to assure Papa that you were a properly serious deputy under secretary of state who would prove a respectable chaperon for my tour."

"I wouldn't think a woman of your vast experience would require a chaperon, Princess."

It would have been impossible to miss the disdain on his face. Obviously, the man had already made up his mind about her, preferring gossip to fact. Well, she decided, if he was expecting the rich, spoiled princess of the tabloids, that's precisely what he'd get.

"You're quite right, Mr. O'Bannion," she said, giving him a calculating smile totally devoid of warmth. "I don't need a chaperon nearly as badly as I need someone to retrieve my luggage." She reached into her black leather clutch, extracted a stack of bright blue cardboard tags and held them out to him. "I assume that's to be your job?" she asked in a haughty tone that one of her ancestors might have used on a recalcitrant footman.

The flare of anger in Caine's eyes would have made a lesser woman flinch. Chantal held her ground, refusing to be intimidated by his blistering scrutiny.

"The limo's parked right outside in the VIP lot," he ground out as he snapped the luggage tags from her fingers. "Mr. Tremayne will be your driver while you're in this country," he said, indicating the smiling man standing beside him. "He'll get you settled in while I collect your bags."

Proper manners, drilled into Chantal by a rigid British governess who'd been with the family for two generations, were nearly her undoing. She started to thank him, then remembered that a princess—at least the type he thought her to be—need not acknowledge any effort on her behalf. "Please don't take all day," she instructed briskly. "Waiting around in limousines is such a dreadful bore."

The back-and-forth motion of his jaw indicated Caine was grinding his teeth. "I'll try not to dawdle, Your Highness."

"See that you don't."

As she walked away, Drew following on her heels, Caine could have sworn he saw an invisible crown perched atop her sleek sable head. Muttering a particularly virulent curse, he headed toward the baggage claim area, deciding

that he'd take a dozen crazed would-be assassins over one
snotty princess any day.

At least the driver was friendly, Chantal considered.
Although his manner had been properly polite, his eyes
had smiled at her in a way that almost made up for Caine
O'Bannion's rudeness. Alone in the back seat of the State
Department limousine, she thought about her reasons for
coming to America. Burke had been the one who insisted
all she needed to lift her spirits was some time away from
Montacroix. An opportunity for a new lease on life. After
giving the matter serious consideration, Chantal had
agreed that a change of scenery might just do her some
good.

The trick had been to find a place that held no painful
memories, something easier said than done. Then the letter had come inviting Montacroix to take part in a cultural exchange program.

The offer, along with an opportunity to raise much-
needed funds for the world's underprivileged children, had
seemed the answer to a prayer. During the six months that
she'd prepared for the exhibit, selecting works from remarkably talented yet still obscure European artists, along
with the appealingly primitive artwork of the children,
she'd managed to go hours, sometimes even days at a time,
without dwelling on the past. By the time she'd boarded
the Air France jet today, she'd felt as if she were standing
on the brink of a bright new life.

And then she'd run smack into Caine O'Bannion and
that cold, hard look of disdain she remembered all too
well. Her husband had perfected that look, wielding it
with brutal efficiency. After her divorce, Chantal had
thought that she'd never have to see that look directed her
way again. Obviously she'd thought wrong.

"Damn," she murmured, leaning her head against the back of the glove-soft leather seat and rubbing her throbbing temples with her fingertips. "What do I do now?"

"Since your welcoming reception at the Montacroix embassy is only a few hours away and you've had a long flight, I'd suggest going straight to the hotel for a nap," a deep voice beside her offered.

Lost in introspection, Chantal had failed to notice Caine's arrival. Now, as she lowered her hands to her lap, she reminded herself that it was important—vital—that she remain calm.

"I do not take naps."

Her tilted, arrogant chin was quintessential princess, but the obvious exhaustion in her eyes and the pallor of her cheeks hinted at something soft and vulnerable lurking beneath that vivid, self-assured exterior. Telling himself that such flights of fancy must be a residual, unexpected side effect of the pain medication they'd pumped him full of last month, Caine shrugged.

"Fine. You can spend the rest of the day hanging up all the clothes you brought with you." He thought of the numerous pieces of Louis Vuitton luggage he and Drew had finally managed to stuff into the roomy trunk of the limousine. "May I ask you a personal question?"

"I suppose that would depend on how personal."

"Did you leave any clothes back at the castle?"

If he'd been anyone else, Chantal would have laughed and confided that Burke had asked her that very same question when he'd driven her to the airport. But her brother's question had been in the vein of good-natured teasing. Caine's was heavy with scorn.

"I am here in America representing my country," she said blandly. "As Montacroix's unofficial delegate to the United States, I have a reputation to uphold."

"Excuse my ignorance, Your Highness," Caine shot back mockingly. "I hadn't realized that an entire country's international reputation depended on the size of its princess's wardrobe."

It crossed Chantal's mind that if Caine O'Bannion was typical of the country's State Department officials, America's foreign affairs were bound to be in a great deal of trouble. She couldn't remember ever meeting a more undiplomatic man.

"Don't tell me that my luggage is too heavy for you to manage?"

"Of course not. However, I *was* wondering whether you plan to lug all those cases around from town to town for the next three weeks."

"Don't be ridiculous. I have no such intention."

That, at least, was something, Caine decided. Obviously, she'd decided to pull out all the stops for the diplomatic circuit, intending to ship a lot of the stuff back home to good old Montacroix before they moved on to their next stop.

"*You're* going to lug them from town to town for the next three weeks," Chantal returned silkily, her tone schooled to annoy.

As she watched the smoldering fury rise in those hard eyes, she swallowed, all too aware of her heart hammering in her throat. Feeling defensive and hating herself for it, she turned away.

Before Caine could come up with an answer that was even remotely civil, she was pointing out the window. "Oh, the Lincoln Memorial," she exclaimed as the limousine sped past on the way to the hotel. "I read in my travel guide that on a clear day you can see Mr. Lincoln's statue in the Reflecting Pool. Is that true?"

The transformation had been so rapid, so unexpected, that Caine was forced to blink slowly to regain his equilibrium. The haughty princess was gone, and in her place was an enthusiastic young woman whose dancing dark eyes could bring even the most stalwart of men to his knees. As he struggled against an unruly tug of attraction, Caine tried to recall the last time he'd stopped to look at any of his adopted city's famed landmarks.

"If it says it in black and white, it must be true."

Chantal was leafing madly through her book while at the same time trying not to miss any of the sights passing by the tinted windows.

"So many statues. My great-grandfather adored statues—he had them built all over Montacroix. There are those detractors of my family who insist that we have more statues in Montacroix than we do citizens, but of course that's an exaggeration. Still, I have to admit that even when driving through the countryside you can't get away from my great-grandfather Leon's statues."

"The pigeons must love him."

Chantal glanced back over her shoulder, surprising him with a saucy grin. "That's the same thing Burke always says."

"Burke is your brother."

"Technically my half brother," she corrected. "His mother was Papa's first wife. Burke was only five years old when my parents fell in love. He was ten when they were finally permitted to marry. Those five years in between were definitely not easy on anyone." She exhaled a soft, rippling sigh. "Divorce is so horrible. I can't imagine what it must be like for a child, having his world turned upside down before he's old enough to comprehend what's happening."

"It sure as hell isn't easy," Caine said, thinking of his own disrupted life.

Something in his gritty tone caught her attention. Interest, along with a surprising hint of sympathy, appeared in her eyes. "Were your parents divorced?"

Caine wondered how the hell they'd gotten started in on his personal life. He was a bodyguard, nothing more. And a reluctant one at that. He had no interest in knowing anything more about Chantal Giraudeau than whatever basic facts he needed to ensure her safety. And he damn well didn't want her knowing anything about his personal life.

"My father died when I was a boy."

"Oh. I'm sorry." Chantal studied him silently. Then, reminding herself that she had no interest in this man other than whether he could effectively manage her travel arrangements, she fell silent, content to simply observe the scenery going by the tinted windows.

Unaccustomed to Washington's streets, Chantal had no way of knowing that the limousine's abrupt turn was taking them in the opposite direction from the hotel. Aware that Drew must have spotted a tail, Caine stiffened, shifted his gaze to the rearview mirror and automatically reached for the gun hidden beneath his jacket.

The tense moment passed as the yellow taxi that had appeared to be following them continued on its way down Connecticut Avenue. Drew returned to their initial route, leaving Caine to breathe a sigh of relief. Within minutes the limousine pulled up in front of the hotel.

As Chantal entered the luxurious lobby, with its gold domed ceiling and gleaming travertine marble floors, she hoped that the check in would be achieved with the Americans' usual display of efficiency. She had no desire to remain with the obviously disapproving Caine O'Bannion any longer than was absolutely necessary.

HER SUITE WAS ROOMY, gracious and full of the small details that made a hotel a pleasure, from the authentic antique furniture to the wide, comfortable bed with goose-down pillows to the basket of imported soaps, lotions and fragrant bath salts. As she toured her spacious quarters, Chantal knew that had it not been for the silent man following her every move, she would have been very comfortable here.

"It's quite lovely," she said after returning to the living room.

She'd tossed her cape onto a chair immediately upon entering the suite, and as Caine observed the stark but obviously expensive black sweater and slacks, he decided that this was a woman who'd look good in anything. Or nothing. Try as he might, he had not been able to get the picture of her lying on the beach, her nearly nude body gleaming with oil, out of his mind.

"I'm glad you approve."

For the sake of peace, Chantal decided to ignore his clipped tone. She also decided that it was time to drop the prima donna princess act. Not only was it exhausting to behave so out of character, she had the impression that Caine was not a man to be easily fooled for long.

"You don't like me very much, do you, Mr. O'Bannion?" she asked as she attempted to untie the ribbon on the enormous cellophane wrapped basket of fruit and cheeses on a nearby table.

Reaching into the pocket of his slacks, Caine pulled out a compact Swiss army knife and deftly dispensed with the ribbon. "I don't know you."

"True." Selecting a peach, Chantal bit into it, savoring the succulent rush of juice. "You don't know me. Nevertheless, you have formed a decidedly negative opinion regarding my character." She plucked a red Delicious apple from the basket. "Would you care for a piece of fruit?"

The way she looked right now—her dark hair in a wild tangle around her shoulders, her full lips glossy with nectar, the ripe, red fruit in her outstretched hand—enabled Caine to have a good idea how Adam must have felt when Eve showed up in the Garden of Eden with the suggestion that they try something different for dessert.

"No, thanks." Caine was trying to relate this self-possessed woman with the devil-may-care princess of the tabloids. Impossible. "You've got a busy night ahead of you. I'd better leave so you can get some rest."

Her early-morning departure, the differences in time zones, jet lag, not to mention the unsettling meeting with Caine, had all conspired to make Chantal suddenly exhausted. "I believe I will take a nap before the reception," she said. "I'm strangely tired."

"I suppose even princesses get jet lag."

She'd been a princess all her life. For the past twenty-four years, discounting those disastrous months of her marriage, she'd lived a life of luxury in the royal palace. Yet, for some reason, the way he insisted on pointing out her position was beginning to grate on her nerves.

"You do know," she said evenly, "that my mother was—and still technically is—an American citizen."

"Of course." Despite all his warnings to himself to keep his distance, Caine smiled. "I remember that no matter where my father was stationed in the world, he never missed a Jessica Thorne film. My mother always accused him of having a crush on her."

"Really." Although she couldn't begin to count the times she'd heard similar declarations, Chantal found herself responding to his sudden grin. He should smile more often, she decided. It made him look warmer. Nicer. More human.

"I can't remember the name of his favorite, but it was the one where she played a mermaid caught in the net of a fisherman in the Greek isles."

"*Siren Song.*"

"That's it. Mom told me about one night when it popped up on the late show and Dad became so enthralled with those scenes of your mother perching atop her rock that Mom threatened to divorce him."

"Surely she wouldn't have done that?"

"Of course not. But the next night, to make up for his perceived indiscretions, he took her out dancing." Caine didn't mention that that was his father's last night stateside before his death.

"*Siren Song* was Mother's last picture. It is also my father's favorite. They met while she was filming it on Mykonos and fell in love at first sight. Rumor has it that the censors didn't know which to be more upset about— her amazingly scanty wardrobe or her heated, offscreen romance with a married prince."

Chantal smiled as she thought about the fairy-tale story of her parents' love affair. A love affair that scandalized European society for five years. "Everyone said it would never last, but they're as much in love today as they were thirty years ago. Perhaps even more." Her eyes turned dreamy. "Papa still calls her his siren. Isn't that amazing?"

Caine realized he was being given a glimpse of yet another Chantal, this one an unabashed romantic. Her open smile enticed him nearer, even as he knew he'd drown in the swirling depths of those mysterious dark eyes. She exuded sensual heat from every pore, making him want to reach out and touch her skin, to discover if it was really as warm as it looked.

"Not so amazing," he said gruffly, "if she's anything like her daughter."

As their eyes met and held, Chantal couldn't have moved if she'd wanted to. Just when she was certain that her heart had stopped beating, a sudden knock on the door shattered the expectant mood.

"That'll be the bellman with your luggage," Caine said.

Chantal wondered if his frown was due to the untimely interruption or the fact that for one suspended moment he'd allowed himself to be as drawn to her as she was to him.

She glanced down at her slender gold wristwatch, but her numbed mind was unable to decipher the Roman numerals. "I hope I still have time to send tonight's evening dress down to be pressed," she murmured, seeking something, anything, to say.

She was obviously flustered and trying not to show it. Her cheekbones were splashed with scarlet and her eyes— those amazing, sultry eyes—were still wide with an enticing blend of confusion and passion. Dragging his gaze from her exquisite face, Caine went to open the door.

"I'm sure you won't have any problem getting someone to press your gown," he said once the bellman had left with a generous tip. "After all, according to the fairy tales, whenever a princess snaps her fingers, her minions immediately scurry to do her bidding."

Well, Chantal considered, sinking onto a gold-brocade-covered Louis XIV chair, the moment, as intriguing and unsettling as it had been, had definitely passed. The old Caine O'Bannion was back. In spades.


IT WAS EARLY MORNING in Montacroix. The streets were silent save for a sleepy shopkeeper taking the shutters from his windows while his wife hosed down their section of cobblestone pavement. A fat cat, the color of old stonework, curled up on a balcony overlooking nearby Lake Losange and took a bath in the first shimmering beam of golden alpine light.

Two men—one in his mid-thirties, the other at least twice that—sat at a wrought-iron table on the balcony, talking quietly over their café au lait. "She has arrived," the younger man said.

The older man nodded. "So it begins. What security have the Americans provided?"

"None."

The older man didn't answer immediately. Instead, he appeared to be mulling over the unexpected news as he lit a cigarette. "That is a surprise."

"A pleasant one."

"Perhaps." The man exhaled a cloud of smoke, watching the slender blue column rise, then dissipate on the crisp air. "The princess is traveling all alone on this cultural tour?"

"Not exactly."

"Aha. I thought not."

"There is a man accompanying her. But he is only a minor diplomat and no threat to us."

"I wonder." The man reached down and stroked the cat's damp, newly bathed fur. In the early-morning silence, the animal's purring sounded like a small, finely tuned motor. "If this American diplomat proves to be a nuisance, he must be eliminated, as well."

"Of course. I've already made provisions for such an eventuality."

"*C'est bon.*" His lips, beneath the salt-and-pepper mustache, curved upward as he lifted his cup in a silent toast.

"This time," the younger man promised, "we will not fail."

Rigid determination hardening their dark eyes, both men's gazes moved to the island in the middle of the diamond-bright lake, where the Giraudeau palace turrets jutted above the mist-shrouded trees.

# 3

THE MONTACROIX AMBASSADOR'S reception for Princess Chantal was the social event of the season. While in other cities wealth might be the key to social success, in the nation's capital, political clout was what counted; tonight, all the heavy hitters were in attendance. Everyone in "The Green Book"—Washington's social register—had been eager to meet the glamorous princess.

And Chantal did not disappoint. She was, quite simply, the most beautiful woman Caine had ever seen. Eschewing the elaborate beading, sequins and chiffon flounces worn by the other women, who seemed grimly determined to outdo one another, Chantal had opted for a strapless, floor-length tube of black satin that captured the light from the crystal chandeliers and gleamed with her every movement.

She'd pulled her thick, dark hair into an elaborate twist at her nape, thus emphasizing her high cheekbones and sultry, dark eyes. An avalanche of milky pearls curved around her neck, tumbling down toward a single, flawless ruby. Enormous blood-red rubies adorned her ears, and a glowing pearl had replaced the canary-yellow diamond on the ring finger of her right hand. She was, Caine noticed, still wearing the thin silver ring.

From the moment she entered the embassy, Chantal was in total control of the situation. As he watched her in the reception line, standing beside the ambassador and his wife, greeting the Washington notables with a graceful warmth that seemed inbred, Caine couldn't help wondering if there was some genetic code that made a princess a princess.

While he admired her behavior, Caine found the ease by which she slipped into a friendly yet vaguely distant regal bearing strangely inhibiting. Although he'd been surprised to discover Chantal to be such a multifaceted woman, thus far he'd been able to deal with all her varied personalities, including the one he most disliked—the pampered prima donna. But the woman he now observed possessed an intrepid self-assurance he knew went all the way to the bone. Gleaming steel wrapped in black satin—that was the princess Chantal.

He felt an unwelcome stir of desire and told himself that it was going to be a very long three weeks.

STRANGE HOW he reminded her so of Burke, Chantal mused later in the evening as she cast a surreptitious glance toward Caine. For a diplomat, he was surprisingly aloof, standing rigidly apart from the others, refraining from entering into any of the obligatory social small talk. And although he hadn't hovered over her, whenever she turned around he was somewhere nearby, watching her with a steadiness that revealed little about his thoughts.

There was nothing relaxed about this man, nothing easy. He was all intensity and intellect. Just like her brother. Chantal wondered if he also possessed Burke's patience and loyalty. And his passion. An image flashed through her mind, a patently erotic image of lovemaking with Caine that caused a quick thrill to race through her, leaving her weak.

Caine saw the color drain from her face to be replaced seconds later by a pair of red flags in her cheeks. Instantly alert, he scanned the crowded room as he deftly wove his way through the guests to her side.

"Are you all right?"

His voice was low, meant only for her ears. The light touch of his fingers on her elbow burned her skin. "Of course," she said.

"Are you sure? You looked as if you were about to pass out."

His tone reflected more than polite concern. Although she had no reason to believe that Caine possessed the gift of second sight, she also knew that it would be impossible to keep anything from him. Those unwavering eyes saw too much.

"Positive." She managed a reassuring smile. "It's been a long day. I probably should not have had so much to drink."

"You've been carrying that same glass of champagne around all night."

They were face-to-face now, their bodies nearly touching, effectively closing out the others.

"You're very observant."

"It's my job to be observant."

"Perhaps." She studied him, all frank eyes and lingering curiosity. "Yet, isn't it also a diplomat's duty to mingle at functions such as these?"

"I suppose you could include that in the job description."

"The Montacroix ambassador has spoken with everyone here tonight," Chantal observed. "I myself have exchanged greetings with representatives of countries I didn't even know existed. But you haven't said a single word to anyone."

There was no way Caine was going to tell her what his usual function at gatherings such as these was. "I'm talking to you."

"I'm the first. And only."

He shrugged. "I guess I'm just antisocial."

She gave him a long, measuring look that had Caine believing the princess was quite possibly more than just another pretty—no, stunning—face.

"Would you consider me rude if I were to suggest that if you really are antisocial, perhaps you should consider another line of work?"

"Such as?"

Chantal toyed with the silver ring on her finger as she looked up at him, carefully framing her answer. "That's difficult to say. . . without knowing you better," she said slowly. "But the first thing that came to mind when I saw you at the airport, then tonight, looking so stern and alert, is that you reminded me of one of my father's palace guards."

His eyes remained remote, his face expressionless. "Now that's an interesting idea. If I were to apply for the position, would I have to wear one of those striped uniforms with pantaloons and a funny plumed helmet?"

"I believe those are the Vatican guards you're referring to," Chantal said. "They're Swiss. We are far more restrained in Montacroix."

"That's a relief. I've never looked all that good in tights."

"'Tights'?" a deep, laughing voice repeated. "Whatever are you two talking about?"

Caine and Chantal turned toward the tall, distinguished-looking man who'd joined them. When they'd been introduced earlier in the evening, Chantal had recognized the name Sebring immediately and had been pleased to meet the man her father had always spoken of so highly.

"I was merely suggesting alternative career choices for Mr. O'Bannion, Mr. Sebring," Chantal answered with a smile.

"'Alternative career choices'?"

"In the event he might ever tire of the State Department."

"Oh?"

"Princess Chantal doesn't believe I have much of a future in the diplomatic corps," Caine said dryly.

"Is that a fact?" The director exchanged a look with Caine. "I do hope Caine hasn't offended you, Princess."

Chantal decided to apply a little diplomacy herself by not bringing up Caine's earlier snide remarks. "Certainly not. Mr. O'Bannion has been the soul of discretion," she said sweetly. "It is simply that he's unlike any other diplomat I've ever met."

"I remind the princess of one of her father's palace guards," Caine offered.

James Sebring's jaw began to twitch. "Is that right?"

"There is a decided resemblance," Chantal replied. "Perhaps if Mr. O'Bannion ever tires of the State Department, he could come to work for you in the Presidential Security."

"Now there's an idea," the director said with forced enthusiasm. "By the way, Princess, my wife and I were discussing the photographs of your paintings in the gallery catalog earlier this evening. She was particularly curious about the inspiration for your most recent work."

As the director deftly steered the conversation onto a safer track, Caine took the opportunity to drift back into the crowd, remaining, as always, only an arm's length from Chantal.

A palace guard, he mused. As he watched her carrying on an obviously stimulating conversation with Sebring, a senior senator from Illinois and a newly appointed Supreme Court justice, Caine wondered if Chantal had any idea how close she'd come to hitting the bull's-eye.

THERE WAS A LIGHT RAIN falling when they left the reception. For the first time since they'd entered the lofty, dignified reception hall of the embassy, Chantal allowed herself to relax. Leaning her head back against the leather seat of the limousine, she closed her eyes.

She was so silent and so still that Caine thought she'd fallen asleep until she said, "I'm famished."

"You should have eaten something at the reception."

"Impossible. Royal etiquette decrees that a princess never eats in front of her public."

"You are kidding."

"Only slightly." Opening her eyes, she met his incredulous look. "Whenever I'm on public display, especially in such a formal setting such as tonight, it's safer to refrain from eating. Think what a disaster it would be if the princess of Montacroix spilled cocktail sauce down the front of her dress. Or worse yet, someone else's gown."

"Probably change the free world as we know it today," Caine agreed dryly. "The dining room is probably closed at the hotel, but there's always room service."

"I'm not certain the room service menu has what I'm hungry for."

Her sultry scent surrounded them in the warm air of the limousine, filling his head. "Don't be ridiculous," Caine countered, reminding himself that she was merely an assignment—an assignment he didn't want. "You're a princess. The chef will undoubtedly be thrilled to whip up anything your royal little heart desires."

Since the scorn seemed to be missing from his tone this time, Chantal decided not to challenge his renewed reference to her royal status. "Do you think he'd be all that eager to grill a cheeseburger?"

"A cheeseburger?"

"With French fries. And lots of catsup. I do believe that cheeseburgers and French fries are one of the best things about America."

Her light laughter made Caine think of silver wind chimes touched by a summer breeze.

"I've tried for years to teach Bernard, our family chef, the way to grill a proper cheeseburger, but he can't seem to manage such a simple task. Although I can't prove it, I believe he refuses to learn out of spite."

"Spite?"

"I'm afraid he's not much of a fan of America," she said on a slight sigh. "Actually, as far as Bernard is concerned, Montacroix is the cradle of civilization. Anyone who is not a citizen of our small country is obviously a barbarian, guilty of all sorts of primitive behavior."

"Such as eating cheeseburgers and French fries."

Chantal nodded. "Exactly." She caught a glimpse of a blue-and-green neon sign flashing outside the limousine window. "The sign says Open 24 Hours," she exclaimed happily. "Driver, please stop here."

Drew, only slowing slightly, lifted his eyes to the rearview mirror. "Mr. O'Bannion?"

Chantal was not accustomed to having her instructions questioned. Especially not by a chauffeur. "Mr. Tremayne," she repeated firmly, in that tone Caine was beginning to recognize, "I asked you to stop."

"I'm sure you'll be able to order a cheeseburger from room service," Caine assured her, waving Drew on with his hand.

Chantal's previously merry eyes flashed with temper. "I'm going to be spending far too much time in hotel rooms as it is during this tour. I wish to eat out tonight." She lifted her chin, daring him to defy her request. "I wish to eat at that restaurant we just passed."

"You know, my grandmother O'Bannion has a saying—if wishes were horses, beggars would ride."

Chantal found herself wishing that she'd been a princess in a former century so she could banish Caine O'Bannion to the dungeons. "What does some ancient family proverb have to do with my dinner?"

"Think about it," Caine suggested. "Besides, that restaurant is nothing but a greasy spoon. The hamburger bun would undoubtedly be dripping in grease, and the coffee would taste like battery acid. We're returning to the hotel."

The dungeons were too good for this arrogant, unpleasant man, she decided. "Precisely the way I like my dinner. Now, are you going to instruct our driver to turn around, or shall I simply return after you take me back to my suite?"

Their eyes met and held; blazing amber eyes dueling with hard gray. Caine tried to remember when he'd run across such a hardheaded woman and came up blank. "Okay, Drew," he said on a frustrated burst of breath, "take the princess back to the damn diner."

Satisfied, Chantal rewarded him with a dazzling smile that didn't quite expunge his irritation but nevertheless managed to ease it a great deal. "Thank you, Mr. O'Bannion," she said. "That's very diplomatic of you."

As the limousine made an illegal U-turn in the center of the nearly deserted street, Caine didn't answer. He didn't dare.

Thirty minutes later, Caine was sitting in a red vinyl booth, looking in awe at Chantal across the scratched and nicked green Formica table. For a princess, there was certainly nothing dainty about her appetite, he considered, watching as she single-handedly made a cheeseburger, a double order of fries and a chocolate milk shake disappear. At the moment, she was debating over dessert.

"I suppose, since I'm in America, I should have the apple pie," she mused aloud. "But the chocolate cake sounds heavenly."

Where did she put it all? As he cast an appraising glance over her slender but oh so pleasingly curved figure, Caine decided that her metabolism must be locked into high gear.

"Why not order them both?"

"What a marvelous idea! I can eat the apple pie now and take the cake back to the hotel for later. Thank you, Mr. O'Bannion. That was a decision worthy of Solomon."

"Not quite, but I'll accept the compliment nevertheless. On one condition."

"Do you think the waitress would be willing to serve the pie à la mode . . . ? What condition is that?"

"You're in luck. Apple pie without vanilla ice cream is unpatriotic. And the condition is that you stop calling me Mr. O'Bannion. The name's Caine."

Chantal nodded. "Caine," she repeated slowly, as if measuring the taste and feel of it on her tongue. "Caine O'Bannion. It's a fine, strong name. I like it."

"I'll tell my mother," he said dryly. "She'll be so happy that you approve."

Chantal refrained from answering immediately, waiting while Caine gave her order to the waitress. She braced her elbows on the table and linked her fingers together, studying him judiciously. "Why do you insist on being so sarcastic," she asked quietly, "when it's not your nature?"

Caine took a sip of his coffee. He'd been wrong; it didn't taste like battery acid. Toxic waste was more appropriate. "What makes you think it's not?"

"The president has been a friend of my family since I was a child. He'd never have requested the State Department to assign you to me if he'd known how rude you'd be. Or how much you were going to dislike me."

"I don't dislike you."

"Don't you?"

"Not at all. Oh, maybe I did at first, when you pulled that little stunt in the airport, but if you want to know the truth, Princess, you're beginning to grow on me."

"Always the diplomat," she murmured.

When he stretched his long legs under the table and brushed hers, Chantal felt a tingle of something indiscernible race through her veins. What was it? Pleasure? Desire? Fear? As she met his unwavering gaze, she reminded herself that just because Caine O'Bannion was different from any man she'd ever met, didn't mean that he was special.

For someone who'd been schooled in royal discretion since birth, Chantal's face was an open book. Caine watched as the emotions washed over her delicate features in waves. When he viewed what could only be fear, he wondered what the hell he'd done to make her afraid of him. Whatever it was, he considered, he'd have to correct things before they got out of hand. Before she called the president and requested that he be replaced.

While trying to think of something to say that would ease the tension hovering over the table, Caine was saved by the waitress returning with Chantal's dessert. Putting his hand over his chipped white mug, Caine turned down the offer of a refill on the toxic waste.

"Montacroix is a constitutional monarchy, isn't it?" he asked in an apparent attempt to change the subject. In truth, he wanted to see if he could determine a reason for the attempts on the princess's life.

"That's right. Besides my father, the country is ruled by the prime minister, a four-member cabinet appointed by the prince, and an eight-member elected parliament."

"The monarchy is always represented by a prince?"

"Succession to the throne is through the male line."

Obviously no one was trying to keep Chantal from ascending the Montacroix throne. "Does that bother you?"

"Does what bother me?"

"That you'll always be merely a princess with ceremonial duties and no real power?"

Chantal laughed. "If you knew my brother, Burke, you wouldn't be asking me that question," she said. "In the first place, I'd never want all the responsibilities he's going to inherit. And in the second place, though I dearly love my country, I'm not certain I wish to spend the rest of my life in Montacroix."

So far everything they'd discussed had been in her file, but this last statement was news. "What's the matter, is

Montacroix getting a little too provincial for you, after all those years of jet-setting around the world?"

Chantal ignored his gritty tone. "Not at all. I love Montacroix, but I have become more introspective as I approach my thirtieth birthday, and lately I've been thinking that since I've spent the first twenty-nine years of my life in my father's country, I should see how I adapt to my mother's homeland."

"I'm afraid there's not a lot of demand for royalty in America, Princess."

Her chin came up. "Has anyone ever told you that you're a very rude man?"

Her annoyance rolled off him as he shrugged. "If by rude you mean I'm not continually tugging my forelock in your presence, I suppose I could plead guilty."

"That's not what I'm talking about," she tossed back on a flare of temper. "I'm referring to the way that you continually insult me for something I have no control over."

They were the only customers in the diner. Realizing that she had drawn the interest of both the bored, gum-chewing waitress and the late-night fry cook, Chantal lowered her voice.

"There are those in Montacroix, even now, who cannot forgive my father for falling in love with my mother. Despite the fact that long before they'd met, the doctors had informed him that his first wife, Princess Clea, would never be sane enough to leave the sanitorium where she'd been a patient for years."

He knew the story, of course. Anyone who didn't know the story of the beautiful love child produced by Prince Eduard and international sex symbol Jessica Thorne would have had to have spent the past three decades camped out on the dark side of the moon. In fact, Caine recalled, a condemnation of the American actress had actually been written into the congressional record by a Mississippi legislator running for reelection on a morality platform.

"I knew that his wife had been hospitalized," Caine said. "I hadn't realized she'd had mental problems."

"According to my father, instability ran in her family. Her mother committed suicide in a mental institution. Princess Clea had been getting progressively worse throughout their marriage. Shortly after Burke was born, she was committed to the sanitorium, where she finally died last year."

"It must have been tough on your father."

"My governess, who was also governess to my father, once told me that life around the palace had been dreadful for a very long time. Which is why I've always been happy he was fortunate enough to receive a second chance at love, despite the fact that even as a child, I heard people whispering about my mother and their affair behind my back. When I was seven, I finally got up the nerve to ask my father what they meant when they referred to me as 'the bastard princess.'"

The sudden surge of tenderness came as a surprise to Caine. Feeling like a first-class heel for causing that haunting shadow to drift into her eyes, he reached out and took her hand in his. The compassionate caring man in him wanted to apologize, to assure her that she didn't have to tell him any of this. The professional in him recognized a possible motive for her sudden rash of "accidents."

"Who are 'they'?"

Distracted by the feel of his thumb tracing slow circles on the delicate skin of her palm, Chantal failed to comprehend Caine's question. "Pardon?"

Her skin was soft, like the underside of camellia petals. And warm. As he watched the need rise in her eyes, Caine's body responded with an answering heat. "The people who talk about you," he said, forcing himself to keep his mind on his assignment. "Who are they?"

The treacherous thumb had moved to the inside of her wrist. Chantal wondered if he could feel the hammering of her pulse. "No one."

Caine was not accustomed to having his concentration sabotaged this way. And he damn well didn't like it. Princess, hell, he decided as he fought the need to drag her out of this tacky diner and into the back seat of the limousine, where he could finally satisfy his taste for those full, dark lips. She was a witch. A siren. For the first time in his life, Caine understood his father's obsession with Jessica Thorne; like mother, like daughter.

"Someone was talking about you," he pointed out, his voice brusque as he struggled to regain control of both mind and body. "And it bothered you enough to ask your father."

It was his curt tone that brought Chantal back to earth with a bang. Fool, she chided herself. She had no doubt that Caine knew exactly what he was doing to her equilibrium and was enjoying himself immensely.

"I don't understand," she said softly, retrieving her hand with a slight tug. "Your duty, as I was led to believe, is merely to see that my upcoming tour goes smoothly. That nothing will happen to embarrass your country."

"That's about it in a nutshell."

"Then why are you so interested in me?"

Good question, Caine acknowledged silently. The pearl on her finger gleamed like white satin, making the narrow silver band beside it appear almost austere. The two pieces of jewelry were as dissimilar as the disparate personalities he'd witnessed. Who the hell was Princess Chantal Giraudeau, really? And why was the answer suddenly so important?

"You're right. My job is simply to take care of your travel arrangements and make certain that you're comfortable."

He was lying. Of that Chantal was certain. *Why* he was lying, she didn't know. "The story of my childhood is not important. I don't know why I brought it up."

"I believe you were attempting to point out that I was no better than those Montacroix citizens who harbored prejudice against an innocent child," Caine said mildly.

He might be rude, but Chantal had to admit that she liked his directness. So unlike a diplomat, she mused yet again. "You can be quite astute when you put your mind to it, Mr. O'Bannion."

"Caine."

She nodded. "Caine. And as it appears that we will be practically living in each other's pockets for the duration of this tour, you must call me Chantal."

Caine had already determined that it was going to take every ounce of his concentration during the next three weeks to keep his professional distance. He wasn't certain he wanted to dispense with yet another barrier.

"I don't know...."

"Please." Although the restraint necessary for a princess had been drilled into her from a tender age, touching came naturally to Chantal. She reached out and touched his arm, feeling the muscle harden involuntarily under her fingertips. "I really will go mad if you insist on calling me Princess for the next three weeks."

Knowing when he was licked, Caine shook his head. "Does anyone ever say no to you?"

Satisfied with having gotten her way and pleased by the reluctant smile curving his grim lips, Chantal grinned. "There are always a few brave souls who attempt it."

"And what happens to them?"

"What else?" she asked, mischief sparkling in her dark eyes. "I have them flogged."

Her throaty laughter tugged at some unseen chord deep inside Caine. "What else?" he muttered as he tossed some bills onto the table and rose to leave.

It was high time he got the princess back to her hotel room before she touched him again and made him forget his lifelong tenet of never mixing work with pleasure.

# 4

CAINE LAY AWAKE for a long time, staring at the ceiling and thinking about the woman sleeping in the adjoining suite. As beautiful as she'd always appeared in the various magazines, the photos didn't begin to do her justice, he mused, remembering the way her dark hair gleamed under the sparkling lights of the embassy's crystal chandelier. Her complexion possessed the smooth, fine glow usually associated with fine porcelain. And those tawny eyes . . . A man could easily drown in those eyes. That is, if he was weak or foolish enough to permit himself to get that close.

Caine had never considered himself either weak or foolish.

Although he had been assigned to the princess to protect her during her stay in America, Caine knew that if he really wanted to keep Chantal from harm, the best way to do it would be to figure out who was staging these so-called accidents. With that in mind, he gave up on sleep. Slipping into a pair of old tennis shorts and a sweatshirt, he took the manila folder out of the closet safe and began reading. . . .

The sun had just barely risen over the horizon, splitting the pearl-gray sky with brilliant shafts of amethyst and gold, when Caine heard movement in the room next to his. Instantly alert, he shoved his feet into a pair of ragged sneakers and reached for his revolver.

Her door opened, then closed. Cracking his own open a fraction of an inch, Caine watched as Chantal pressed both palms against the wall of the hallway, then stretched the long, taut muscles of her calves. A moment later, she entered the elevator and was gone.

Cursing himself for not knowing about the princess's exercise habits, Caine was out the door in a flash, headed for the stairway.

Chantal smiled as she ran through the peaceful neighborhood. She knew that soon there would be noisy traffic on the street and the sidewalks would be crowded with harried pedestrians making their way to work. But now, in this early-morning light, there were only a few other people stirring. An elderly woman walked an overweight dachshund. A young man in helmet and racing pants madly peddled his bicycle as if he were toning up for the Tour de France. A delivery truck bearing the name Martini's Fresh Fish turned up an alley to deliver seafood to a Spanish restaurant; when the driver rolled down his window and wolf whistled, Chantal decided that some things about America were rather nice.

She'd been running about twenty minutes, checking her time on the diver's watch Burke had given her for her last birthday, when she saw him out of the corner of her eye. A man. A tall, dark-haired man who seemed to be following her.

Chantal increased her pace. Glancing sideways into a shop window, she noticed that the man, without any overt effort, speeded up, as well.

She slowed. The stranger followed suit.

Although she'd never considered herself a hysterical sort of woman, Chantal realized her heart was pounding in her ears. Deciding that discretion was the better part of valor, she turned down an alley, looking for someplace to hide.

Caine was mentally cursing a blue streak as he watched her turn into the narrow alley. Running alone on the streets of any major metropolitan city was foolhardy; taking off down alleys in this neighborhood was downright suicidal.

He'd barely entered the alley himself when Chantal suddenly stepped out from behind an enormous orange dumpster. "It's you!"

Caine stopped dead in his tracks. "What the hell are you doing out here?" he demanded, grabbing her shoulders.

Chantal jerked free of his hold. "What does it look like?" she snapped back, as bewildered by his behavior as she was angry. "I'm running. As you undoubtedly know since you've been following me for at least three blocks."

"Following you? Princess, your paintings must really be something to see, because you have one wild imagination."

Although he tried telling himself that the only reason he hadn't spotted her was that he hadn't expected her to hide behind a trash can, such a feeble explanation didn't ease his feeling of self-disgust. If he'd been this careless two months ago, the president would be lying under an eternal flame at Arlington National Cemetery. Caine didn't know who he was angrier at: Chantal for risking her life this way or himself for not doing a proper job of protecting her.

They were nose to nose, close enough for Chantal to see the blazing fury in his eyes. Along with the anger was another emotion that she could not quite discern. She was not allowed to dwell on it, because as he glared down at her, Chantal experienced a quick flash of desire so hot, so strong that it left her stunned.

Reminding herself exactly who—and what—she was, she wrapped herself in the emotional cloak she had learned to don whenever her fellow students at her private Swiss boarding school had begun whispering behind her back.

"I suppose it is my imagination that you and I just happen to be running on the same street...at the same time?"

Her jaw was jutting out and her back was ramrod straight. A dangerous tempest swirled in her eyes, daring him to lie. Caine wondered if she would be as passionate in bed as she was at this moment and decided that with the right man, she just might be.

"Coincidence is a funny thing," he said with a half shrug.

"Coincidence."

Caine was beginning to wish he'd opted for the CIA instead of Presidential Security after his stint in the navy. He might have gotten killed trying to pull off a dangerous covert operation in some godforsaken country, but at least he would have learned how to come up with an acceptable cover story.

"I run every morning. This is the logical route from the hotel."

Her eyes were still stormy, but now Caine could see a growing seed of doubt in them, as well. "I suppose you could be telling the truth."

"Of course I am. Why would I lie?"

Chantal frowned as she considered his question. "Why, indeed?" she murmured.

"And now that we've had a little breather, how about I accompany you back to the hotel?"

With her long stride she easily kept up with him as they ran back the way they'd come.

As they approached the hotel, Caine noticed a nondescript brown sedan parked across the street, the face of the driver hidden by the pages of the *Washington Post* he was reading. Although he couldn't swear to it, Caine was certain that he'd seen that same car parked in the identical spot when they'd returned from the reception last night. Making a mental note of the license plate, he decided to have Drew run a check. Just in case.

THE SOARING, ANGULAR East Building of the National Gallery of Art was a dazzling example of artistic inspiration. Inside was an explosion of space and light: marble staircases, flying bridges. A vast skylight floated high overhead like a shimmering cloud, flooding the building with sunlight, creating a kaleidoscope of constantly changing colors on the pink marble floors and walls. A bright and whimsical tapestry reflecting Miró's fanciful vision of woman spilled some thirty feet down the central court's south wall.

The gallery had been designed, not as some dark and formal place where visitors would be intimidated, but as intimate rooms where one was invited to absorb the art.

After all the effort she'd put into the Modern Images of Europe exhibit, Chantal had been gratified to see that the works had attracted a crowd of both Washingtonians and tourists.

"It appears that you're a hit, Princess," Caine observed as they sat over sandwiches and coffee in one of the gallery's cafés. Although it had taken some coaxing, he'd finally managed to pry Chantal away from a clutch of adoring art fans who seemed to be every bit as fascinated by this real-life princess as they were by the paintings she'd brought to this country with her.

"They're marvelous works," she said, beginning to relax for the first time since she'd entered the building. "More than capable of attracting crowds even without my participation. And, of course, the children's artwork always receives rave reviews."

"You can't deny you're an added draw."

"Now you sound like my father. He was the one who insisted that I come to America after learning about the cultural exchange program. He said that as the family's resident artist, it was only proper that I represent Montacroix."

Caine wondered what Chantal would say if she knew that the real reason for her father wanting her to come to America was to get her out of harm's way. Away from whoever it was who was threatening her life.

"I suppose this is where I tell you that I'm impressed by your own paintings." Although what little Caine knew of painting came from an art history class he'd taken in his plebe year at Annapolis, even he could tell that Chantal possessed an enormous gift.

There were three of her works exhibited, the first two abstracts done in primary colors that were so vivid, so filled with joie de vivre that it would have been impossible to keep from smiling while viewing them. The third, however, was the one that the director's wife had obviously been inquiring about at the reception a couple of nights ago. It was as different from the others as night from day.

"Thank you."

"May I ask a question?"

"Of course."

"Why did you paint that third painting?"

Chantal had known all along that it had been a mistake to include that particular painting in the exhibition. But Noel had insisted that by allowing others to view the painting Chantal had done immediately after her separation from her husband, she would finally succeed in exorcising the man as well as the disastrous experience from her life. When Chantal had continued to waver, Burke stepped in, agreeing with Noel, and soon Chantal found herself relenting under the velvet steamroller of her sister and brother's united front.

"Why does any artist paint anything?" she asked with a careless shrug, turning to gaze out the window over the vast green expanse of the Mall. A young man clad in jeans and a Washington Redskins T-shirt was tossing a Frisbee to his Irish setter. But Chantal was only vaguely aware of the dog and his owner as she sought to soothe the panic that had suddenly begun to pound in her head. "It was simply a creative impulse. Nothing more."

"It must have been a pretty grim impulse." The beautiful but cold and stark winter landscape, done in shades of gray and black, double matted in white and framed in cool, polished aluminum, lacked the vivid colors that made the first two paintings such a delight to view.

For not the first time, Chantal wondered what it was about Caine that had her telling the truth when a polite little lie would do. "It was."

"You know," he suggested mildly, "if you're not prepared to talk about it, perhaps you should pull that particular painting from the exhibit."

His tone was so calm, so damn self-assured. Chantal waited for the annoyance, vaguely surprised when it didn't come. "Noel and Burke talked me into it. They said it would do me good."

Caine found it interesting that anyone could talk this woman into doing anything. "And?"

She glanced down at her watch. It was fashioned of antique gold pounded wafer thin. "Really, Caine, I believe it's time I returned to the exhibit."

Recognizing the emotional barriers she was erecting between them, Caine realized he had two choices: he could either skirt them or charge right through. Although he'd always considered himself a proponent of the direct approach, he decided that perhaps in this case, diplomacy might achieve the desired results.

"Anything you say, Your Highness," he agreed easily.

Chantal searched his impassive face, looking for a sign of humor at her expense. Finding none, she rose from the table and started toward the door.

She'd dressed in a bolero jacket and slim-skirted dress of scarlet silk that had made her stand out in a room of pretty spring pastels. But as Caine followed her out of the café, watching the pleated peplum skirt sway with the smooth movement of her hips, he decided that Drew was right—the princess could probably wear a burlap bag and still be the sexiest, most desirable woman he'd ever seen.

He spent the next few hours suffering that now-familiar pull of sexual attraction that occurred whenever Chantal was near and trying to forget that puzzles—all kinds—had always fascinated him.

LATE THAT AFTERNOON Drew informed him that the brown sedan had been a rental. The papers had been signed by a Max Leutwiler, an officer of Crédit Suisse in Geneva.

"So the car's clean," Caine mused.

"Seems to be," Drew agreed.

Although he could think of no reason why a Swiss banker would want to harm Chantal, a little voice in the back of Caine's mind was telling him that something about the situation didn't quite ring true. "Let's run a check on this Leutwiler guy," he said.

Drew had worked with Caine long enough to trust his friend's instincts. "I'll get on it right away."

That evening, as they left for a dinner at the White House, Caine looked for the car. When it wasn't there, he told himself that he should have been relieved. But he wasn't.

LATER THAT NIGHT, across the street from the hotel, two men—one blond and bearded, the other dark and clean shaven—sat in the rented sedan, watching Chantal's window as they drank coffee from plastic foam cups.

"Her lights just went out."

"And O'Bannion has not left the hotel. Again." The gravelly voice was thick with scorn.

"Perhaps he's acting as a bodyguard."

"Don't be naive. In the first place, there's been no sign that anyone suspects that the bastard princess's recent incidents have been anything more than a rash of unfortunate accidents. And in the second place, when I telephoned the State Department this afternoon and asked to speak to Mr. O'Bannion, I was told that he's currently on assignment." The dark-haired man cracked open a window and lit a cigarette. "Diplomats make poor bodyguards."

Although the days were growing warmer, the nights were still tinged with the chill of winter. The bearded man turned his coat collar up around his ears and hunched lower in his seat as the cold came whistling through the open window. "Do you think they are having an affair?"

The other man uttered a sound of sheer disgust. "What do you think?"

"I think that I would like to trade places with O'Bannion, for just one night."

"Don't get any ideas. You are not being paid to spice up your sex life."

"So what's wrong with mixing a little pleasure with business? So long as I get the job done?"

"It's not in the plan."

"Hey, you're the boss," the bearded man said. "Forget I mentioned it." As he returned his attention to Chantal's darkened window, his teeth gleamed in the darkness. "Soon," he murmured under his breath.

"Soon," his companion agreed, flipping his cigarette out the window. The tip gleamed in a sparkling red arc for an instant before being doused in a puddle.

CAINE WAS SIFTING through Chantal's file, searching for some clue he'd overlooked, when the strident ringing of the telephone shattered the predawn silence.

"O'Bannion."

"Caine," James Sebring said without preamble, "you and Chantal have company."

Instantly alert, Caine reached for the shoulder holster he'd put on the end table immediately upon entering the room. "What kind of company?"

"All we know is that a man called the State Department late this afternoon, asking for you."

"And?"

"The receptionist confirmed that you were on assignment."

"That satisfied him?"

"For now." There was a moment's hesitation. "Caine, be careful. I wouldn't want your mother receiving a posthumous medal for you in another rose garden ceremony."

"That makes two of us," Caine agreed. "Don't worry, sir. If it looks as if Drew and I can't handle this alone, I'll request additional help."

"You do that," the director answered promptly. Once he considered a problem taken care of, he was able to put it behind him and get on with other matters. For a man responsible for the safety of the president and vice president, their families, former presidents, their wives and children, major presidential and vice presidential candidates, not to mention visiting heads of state and distinguished foreign visitors, such an attitude was imperative. "By the way, how are you and Chantal getting along?"

"She's an interesting woman," Caine hedged.

"'Interesting.'" The director chortled. "That's one word for her, I suppose, although not the one I would have used. Has she thrown you any curveballs yet?"

"None that I can't handle, sir."

"Just hang in there and keep swinging," he advised.

"Yes, sir."

"You'll be certain to keep me informed about anything suspicious, won't you, Caine?"

"That goes without saying, sir."

"Good. Good. And meanwhile, Prince Eduard's men are working to uncover something in Montacroix, but so far, they keep running into dead ends. Damn, if we could just come up with a motive, we might know where to start looking."

"Have they spoken with her former husband?"

"Of course. He's currently in Africa, preparing for some Saharan road race. From what I'm told, the scoundrel is too busy romancing the ladies to worry about killing his ex-wife. What time do you leave for New York?"

"Ten-thirty."

"Call me when you land. We're still trying to trace that call to the State Department. Perhaps we'll have some luck."

Caine agreed, said goodbye, then hung up. Then he returned to the file, looking for the single clue that would ensure Chantal's safety.

DURING THE NEXT TEN DAYS, as the exhibit moved from Washington to New York, Chantal and Caine fell into an easy routine. She insisted on beginning each day with a morning run, so he always stopped by her hotel room door shortly before seven, prepared to accompany her through the nearby neighborhood.

Although Chantal steadfastly refused to believe her father and brother's assertion that she was in any danger, she couldn't deny that after her initial fright that first morning, she found Caine's company vaguely reassuring. Not to mention that the sight of his strong legs clad in a well-worn pair of white shorts, hard thigh muscles flexing with each stride, was more stimulating than a dozen cups of coffee.

Following the invigorating exercise, they'd go their separate ways again, meeting an hour later for their drive to the museum, where Chantal would spend yet another exhausting day holding court over the Montacroix exhibition. As he watched her standing hour after hour on those ridiculously high heels, ever smiling, Caine decided that being a princess might just be a tougher job than he'd first believed.

During those long days when he remained nearby, watching over her like a Praetorian guard, Caine attempted to unravel the mystery of Chantal's potential assassins. While he had not been at all surprised to learn that there actually was a Max Leutwiler working at Crédit Suisse, neither had it come as any revelation that the good banker was still in Geneva, where he'd been every day for the past three months. Obviously, the car parked outside Chantal's hotel had been rented by an imposter.

But who was he? And where was he? And when was he going to make his move?

Those questions tormented Caine every hour of the day and into the night, when over dinner in some out-of-the-way place—Chantal, to his surprise, consistently eschewed all the "in" restaurants—he'd carefully pump her for information about her life in Montacroix, trying to find something that might provide a clue.

"I believe it's going well, all things considered, don't you think?" she asked on their last night in New York. After a somewhat heated discussion over whether Tex-Mex qualified as authentic Hispanic fare—Caine insisted it didn't, while Chantal's ubiquitous tour book recommended it highly—they'd settled on a cozy Mexican restaurant in the heart of the theater district.

"Better than well. If you pull in a third as many people in the rest of the cities, you can consider your tour a smashing success."

"Please," she murmured, rolling her eyes toward the ceiling, "let's not talk about the upcoming travels."

"You sound tired."

"I am, a bit."

"It's no wonder, considering the grueling hours you've been putting in. Personally I'm surprised that your lips haven't frozen into that royal smile."

"You mean they haven't?" Chantal asked with mock surprise.

"Not yet. You know, I really am impressed."

"Oh?"

"You're not at all what I expected," Caine admitted.

"Ah, yes. That pleasure-seeking princess of the tabloids."

Although Caine would never consider himself guilty of stereotyping, he couldn't deny that he always felt more comfortable when he could categorize people. In a way, his work encouraged such a habit; on more than one occasion, he'd utilized the FBI's assassin profile to uncover some potentially dangerous crackpot.

"I knew they were probably exaggerating," he said on a half shrug, "yet—"

"Where there's smoke, surely there must be fire," Chantal finished for him.

Caine was uncomfortable, which was a distracting feeling for him. He was accustomed to being in control of both mind and body. Yet lately, his mind—both waking and sleeping—had been filled with thoughts of Chantal. And if that wasn't bad enough, he thought as her tongue gathered in a few of the salt crystals garnishing the rim of her glass, desire kept slamming into him.

"Tell me about your marriage," he said, struggling to turn the conversation back to his mission.

He'd already determined that the male ascendancy rule kept her from being a threat to anyone not wanting a Giraudeau on the throne. And his confidential report gathered by intelligence sources in Montacroix had stated that although a few old-timers resented her mother's affair with the prince, everyone in the country appeared genuinely fond of their headstrong, glamorous princess.

It was then Caine had thought of her race car driving husband. What if he was the dangerous type who refused to let go?

His reference to her ill-fated marriage coming as a complete surprise, Chantal paused in the act of tugging a cheese-covered chip from a mountain of nachos. "Why on earth would you want to know about that?"

"You're the one who doesn't want me to think you're the princess in the papers," he pointed out. "I'm just attempting to separate fact from fiction."

"My marriage was a mistake."

"So are fifty percent of the ones in this country. But they don't receive nearly so many headlines."

"Why do I have the feeling that there's more to your question than mere curiosity?"

"Beats me."

She'd managed to extricate the chip and took a bite, eyeing Caine thoughtfully as she chewed. "All right, among other things, Greg Masterson was a pathological liar. In the beginning, I was too infatuated with him to notice the warning signs. Later, I developed sort of a built-in radar, like those—what do they call them—those instruments that sense earthquakes."

"Seismographs."

Chantal nodded. "That's it. I possess a very accurate internal seismograph, Caine. And at this moment its needle is going off the chart."

"That's ridiculous."

"Is it?"

"All right," Caine hedged, wondering exactly how to squirm out of this one. "It's more of a half-truth. Sort of a white lie."

During his childhood years, first his father, then later the nuns at Saint Gregory's Catholic School, had punished him severely every time he'd attempted to tell a lie. Being a bright kid who caught on fast, Caine had decided that it was easier and a great deal less painful to stick to the truth. The outcome of such youthful lessons was that Caine was a lousy liar. Yet in the past ten days, he'd probably been forced to tell more falsehoods than he had in his entire thirty-three years.

"'A white lie,'" Chantal repeated, her tone inviting elaboration.

"I was just trying to figure out what kind of damn fool would let you get away," he said, surprised to discover as he heard the words leave his lips that there was more truth to the quickly thought up explanation than he had intended.

His tone, gruff with the desire he'd been trying to conceal, gave the proper veracity to his words. As she stared across the table at him, Chantal felt that same draining weakness she'd experienced too many times to count.

"That's a very nice thing to say," she managed, her own voice husky as she struggled to clear it.

"It's the truth."

Chantal would have found his words far more encouraging if he hadn't looked so angry. "So you are attracted to me. I'd wondered."

Caine knew it would be futile to lie. "What man wouldn't be?" he returned with forced casualness. "You're beautiful, intelligent, albeit a bit stubborn—"

"I prefer tenacious," Chantal murmured.

"Stubborn," Caine insisted. "Hardheaded. Like a Missouri mule."

"A Missouri mule?" she inquired, allowing herself to be sidetracked by a reference she didn't understand. "This is a new American expression to me. Why not a Washington mule? A Kansas mule? Or even a Montacroix mule?"

"Hey, it's just a saying, okay? I don't have any idea where it came from."

"Perhaps they raise a great many mules in the state of Missouri," Chantal suggested helpfully.

"Perhaps that's it. The point I was making, before I was interrupted—" Caine was cut off by the arrival of the waiter with their main course.

"You were saying?" Chantal asked once they were alone again.

"I was just attempting to explain that any man would be attracted to a woman like you," he said gruffly.

"But some men would not be happy about it. You are not happy about it."

He put down his fork to meet her strangely vulnerable gaze. "Look, Chantal, it's nothing personal."

"It's not?"

Damn, she definitely wasn't making this easy for him. "Of course it's not. Whatever I feel for you—"

"And I for you," she interjected quietly.

"Whatever we feel, the fact remains that we live in two different worlds. You're a princess, for crying out loud, and I'm just a, uh, deputy under secretary of state."

Her dark eyes displayed hurt. "I did not realize that Americans believed in class distinctions."

"We don't, but—"

"Yet," she continued gravely, her eyes not leaving his, "you are willing to turn your back on whatever is happening between us because of artificial barriers."

"They're not artificial," he insisted.

How could she not see that they came from different worlds? Different universes. His days consisted of long, often boring work, and although traveling with the president of the United States had its moments, his life was far removed from the glitter and wealthy circles a princess moved in. He lived in a comfortable, two-bedroom apartment in one of the city's more eclectic neighborhoods; she resided in a palace. He made a decent living; her jewels alone were worth more than the entire treasuries of most Third World nations.

"Your food's getting cold," he pointed out, looking at her untouched plate of enchiladas, tacos, rice and refried beans.

"I'm suddenly no longer hungry."

"Now that's a first."

"As you so succinctly pointed out," Chantal said, "I'm full of surprises." Rising from the table, she marched out of the restaurant, leaving Caine to follow.

The ride back to the hotel was a silent one. A short, intermittent rain had begun during their dinner, and the only sound in the limousine was the swish-swish of the wipers as they brushed the water off the windshield.

"Aren't you at all curious?" she asked finally.

"Curious?"

They'd stopped at a red light. Chantal's head was turned away, her gaze directed toward the rain-washed sidewalk where a man and woman were kissing under the protection of a wide black umbrella. As she watched the tender lovers so oblivious to the outside world, Chantal felt a sharp stab of envy like nothing she'd ever known.

"I've been wondering for days what it would be like to kiss you," she said. Her soft voice was little more than a whisper but easily heard in the intimate confines of the limousine.

"I suppose it's a natural enough curiosity."

"Then you have also wondered?"

Caine shrugged. "Of course. You're a remarkably enticing woman, Princess. Any man would be tempted to kiss you."

"Yet you're not a man to easily succumb to temptation, are you, Caine?"

"No. I'm not."

He was an absolute paragon of restraint. Chantal found herself admiring Caine even though his rigid self-control was driving her crazy. She sighed softly. "Then I'm afraid we have a slight problem."

"What's that?"

"Unlike you, I've always believed in following my instincts. And to tell the truth, I'm not certain I can get through another night without knowing."

As the light turned green and the car started through the intersection, she leaned toward Caine, her eyes gleaming with sensual intent.

# 5

MUTTERING A SOFT OATH, Caine succumbed to the inevitable as Chantal brushed her lips lightly against his, tasting, testing.

She had thought she'd known what Caine's kiss would be like, but as he drew her closer, she realized that even her most vivid fantasy paled in the face of reality.

It wasn't that his mouth was harsh or impatient. To her surprise, he made no attempt to rush them into quick intimacy. When the tip of his tongue circled her parted lips, she sighed. When his teeth nibbled enticingly at her lower lip, she trembled. And when he slipped his tongue between her lips to touch hers, she sighed again and shuddered.

Chantal had grown up in the lap of wealth and privilege. Never had she known need. Until now. As every tingling nerve ending in her body became focused on her mouth, on the sheer glory Caine was capable of bringing to a mere kiss, Chantal, for the first time in her life, experienced true hunger.

"Well? Is your curiosity satisfied?" he asked, nibbling gently on her earlobe.

"Oh, not yet." Her hands went to either side of his face, drawing his lips back to hers. "More."

"Anything you say, Your Highness," he said against her mouth. He'd tried to resist her and failed. Now the only thing to do was to accept this for what it was—an exceptional, once-in-a-lifetime experience—then get on with his life.

A longing slowly built up inside Chantal as Caine kissed her with a patience that made her bones melt. His lips plucked at hers, tenderly, teasingly, before skimming up her face, leaving sparks on every inch of heated skin: the crest of her cheekbones, her eyelids, her temples, her chin. When his treacherous mouth loitered at the base of her throat, she heard a slow, drugged moan of pleasure and realized that it had escaped her own tingling lips.

Clouds covered her mind as he murmured to her, quiet, enticing words that thrilled her as she felt them being formed against her mouth. Degree by glorious degree he deepened the kiss until what had once been soft and gentle grew more demanding.

It was torture. Ecstasy. It was torment. Bliss. The rainy world outside the limousine tilted, then slowly slipped away as Chantal's attention centered solely on Caine's sinfully talented lips. It was as if he meant to kiss her endlessly, and as her avid mouth clung to his, Chantal prayed he'd never stop.

He'd thought he was safe. What harm could there be in a simple kiss? All right, Caine allowed, so it wasn't a simple kiss, but hadn't he realized that would be the case? There hadn't been anything simple about the Princess Chantal yet, so why should he have expected this to be any different? As he felt her skin heating to his touch, felt her warm, soft lips move hungrily, almost desperately against his, he felt himself slowly, inexorably sinking into quicksand.

He'd kissed other women before. More than he could count. But as he kissed Chantal, all those other faces and names blurred into an indistinct, distant memory. He'd wanted other women before, but as an outrageous need to strip off her clothing and taste every fragrant inch of warm, satiny skin—to absorb her—raced through him, Caine knew that no other woman had ever made him burn this way. No other woman had ever made him weak.

Whether he wanted to admit it or not, the princess was like no woman he'd ever met. And that, Caine acknowledged grimly, was precisely what made her so dangerous.

When he realized that they were pulling up in front of the hotel, Caine allowed himself one more lingering kiss, savoring the sweet taste of her lips. That was it, he vowed. That was as far as he could go without getting in over his head.

"I'll see you to your room."

"Yes." Her wide, passion-laced eyes met his, handing him a gilt-edged invitation he was determined to ignore.

As much as he warned himself not to touch her, Caine's hand rested on her back as they rode up in the elevator. Her white cashmere coat was soft; Caine suspected that her skin would be softer.

"Amazing," she murmured, luxuriating in the possessive touch of Caine's hand against her back.

He was a strong man. She'd seen his strength each morning as they ran, witnessed the play of rigid muscles, the power of his long, sinewy legs. But she'd suspected that he could be gentle, as well. And the exquisite tenderness of his kiss had been proof of that. Strength and tenderness—an irresistible combination for any woman, but especially for Chantal. She had waited her entire life for such a man.

He twined his fingers in her hair, tempted to press his lips against the gleaming, dark strands. "What's amazing?" The hell with it, he decided, giving in to temptation. There were still fifteen floors to go; plenty of time to regain his willpower.

Chantal sighed with pleasure as his warm breath fanned her temple. "I was exhausted earlier, yet now..." Her voice drifted off, her dark eyes enticed, her slightly parted lips seduced. "You must be a magician."

Standing close to her as he was, Caine could not avoid meeting her gaze. Thoughts—all of them erotic, each of them dangerous—raced through his mind. Images of hot, humid nights, cool jazz and steamy sex. Of laughing, lazy sex in flower-strewn meadows, while the summer sun smiled benevolently overhead. Lying beside her in a mountain cabin, in front of a crackling fire, her naked flesh gleaming with the reflected orange glow of the firelight as they created a storm that made the blizzard outside pale in comparison.

Princess Chantal was temptation incarnate. A temptation he was finding more and more difficult to resist.

"Not a magician," he said, backing off slightly and shoving his hands into his pockets. "Just a man."

The passion was still there. She could feel it surrounding them, pulsing beneath her skin, like a thousand live wires. But now there was something else, as well. Something she reluctantly acknowledged as she watched the shield close over his smoky gray eyes. "A man determined to resist my feminine charms."

Caine read the hurt in her eyes and realized what a challenge it must have been for her to pull off that casual, teasing tone. "Chantal—" He reached for her, but she backed away, shaking her head.

"No," she insisted on a voice that wavered only at the edges. "Don't make things worse by apologizing, Caine." She gave him a smile—a brave, trembling smile that tore at something deep inside him. "I've always been impulsive. It's one of my more unattractive traits—"

"I doubt that there's anything unattractive about you."

At the moment, when she was struggling to hang on to one last shred of dignity, Chantal did not welcome his kindness. "Please," she said, pressing her fingers against his lips, "don't say anything. Not until I finish."

Caine nodded.

Drawing in a deep breath that was meant to calm but didn't, Chantal tried again. "Despite what you've read of my alleged romantic escapades, the truth is that I've never been very good at relationships," she began quietly. "Something—or someone—always seems to get in the way."

She thought of the various individuals she'd given her heart to, only to learn the hard way that too many men received an ego boost from attracting—then subsequently dumping—a princess. Even those not attracted by her title had found her wealth irresistible, courting her by day even as they spent their nights with beautiful, sexually hedonistic women who were not foolish enough to expect love or commitment in return.

Perhaps, she considered, it was she who was wrong. Perhaps it was not that the men in her life had promised too little, but that she had expected too much.

"What I'm attempting to say," she continued falteringly, "is that if you walk away from me tonight, I'll live. It won't be the first time a man has rejected me, and I doubt that it will be the last. But—" she took a deep breath "—if you are at all tempted to seize the moment, so to speak, I would not send you away."

As he watched the vivid color bloom in her cheeks, Caine realized that the princess, who had displayed amazing composure under some very trying conditions, was more than a little embarrassed by this intimate conversation.

"I can't think of anything I'd rather do than make love to you," he said honestly.

"But . . . ?"

"I thought I had explained all that."

"The part about us coming from different worlds."

The elevator door opened onto her floor, and although Caine was tempted to ride down to the parking garage and back up again all night long if that's what it took to get this settled, he didn't trust himself to be alone in such a confined space with a woman whose very scent drove him to distraction.

"Exactly." Putting his hand under her elbow, he guided her out into the hallway.

Chantal was quiet as they walked the short distance to her door. She was not in the habit of offering herself to a man, and although Caine's rejection stung, she wasn't about to let him see he had the capacity to hurt her.

Relieved when she appeared willing to allow the matter to drop, Caine escorted her into the room as he did every night, his swift, surreptitious gaze sweeping the suite. The day before their arrival, he'd arranged for her doors and windows to be wired to an alarm system that sounded both in his room and in the manager's office downstairs. If anyone had broken in during their absence, he or Drew would have been informed of the fact by the desk clerk. But it still didn't hurt to double-check.

"I'll want to run in the morning, before the flight," she said, shrugging out of her coat. The snowy cashmere fell unheeded onto the plush carpeting.

"You really do look tired," he said, noticing for the first time the pale blue shadows under her eyes. He picked the coat up and tossed it over the arm of a nearby chair, noting as he did so that it carried her scent. "Perhaps you should sleep in."

She kicked off her high heels as she headed for the bedroom. "All I need is a good night's sleep. I have no intention of foregoing my run tomorrow. If you're not here, I'll simply go alone." Her back was to him, and as she pulled down the zipper of her black silk dress, Caine was treated to a generous expanse of creamy flesh.

Biting down a surge of desire so strong that it was all he could do not to toss her onto that king-sized bed, Caine opted to leave now, while he still could. "Hey, Princess."

"Yes?" She turned in the bedroom doorway.

"Anyone ever tell you that there are times a guy might just mistake you for a Missouri mule?"

Fluttering her dark lashes, Chantal gave him a saucy, impertinent Gypsy's smile. "Only one man. But since I have reason to question his judgment, I choose not to believe him. *Au revoir*, Caine. I will see you in the morning. Early." Flashing yet another smile even more tantalizing than the first, she shut the bedroom door between them.

As he entered the room he shared with Drew, it crossed Caine's mind that she wasn't the only one questioning his judgment. How many men would have turned down what the princess was offering this evening?

"DON'T SAY A WORD," he warned as he encountered Drew's knowing grin. An instant before that heated kiss, it had occurred to Caine the partition was open and Drew could see them in the rearview mirror. But then her lips had touched his and coherent thought had fled his mind. "Not one single word."

"About what?" Drew asked with feigned innocence.

Caine was about to reply when the telephone rang. "Yeah," he answered abruptly, not bothering to conceal his irritation.

"Mr. Caine O'Bannion?" The hesitant feminine voice, faint, as though coming over long-distance lines, caught him by surprise. Besides the hotel manager, only two people—Director Sebring and the president—knew he was staying at this hotel.

"Sorry, wrong number," he said.

"Mr. O'Bannion, please don't hang up. This is Noel Giraudeau. Chantal's sister."

"Chantal?"

"Oh, please, let us not waste time with foolish games. Not when Chantal is in such grave danger." Her voice was calm, but Caine could detect an undercurrent of fear.

"Look, Princess—"

"Please, call me Noel," she interjected.

"The thing is, I have no idea who or what you're talking about. Besides which, I'm a little busy right now. If you really want to talk, I'll have to get back to you, okay?"

"But..." Her voice drifted off. "I see," she said thoughtfully. "That is very clever, Mr. O'Bannion. I should have realized that you would want to confirm that I am who I say I am before talking with me. Papa says the president assured him that you're exemplary at your job."

Instinct, along with the mention of the president, told Caine that this woman was exactly who she said she was. Experience kept him cautious.

"I'll call you when I have more time to talk."

"Of course," she agreed smoothly. "I'll be waiting for your call, Mr. O'Bannion."

Caine hung up, exchanged a look with Drew as he counted to ten, then dialed the private number he'd been given upon accepting this assignment.

Noel Giraudeau answered on the first ring. "You're very prompt, and cautious. You've no idea how that eases my mind, Mr. O'Bannion."

Her voice was a great deal like her sister's, but more restrained, more soothing. From the file photos, Caine had deduced that pretty, ice-blond Noel was cool to Chantal's hot.

"I'm glad to hear that," he said sincerely. "Is that what you were calling for? To check me out?"

"Gracious, no." She sounded flustered. "You come highly recommended. I wouldn't think—"

"Then why did you call?"

"To beg you to stop Chantal from going to Philadelphia tomorrow morning."

"You of all people must know that it's difficult to get your sister to do anything she doesn't want to do," Caine pointed out. "And of all the cities on the tour, she's looking forward to Philadelphia the most."

He didn't bother to add his irritation about her sudden, last minute decision this afternoon to stay at the home of an old friend. The hotel they'd booked was secured; he and Drew had seen to that. Her friend's house, on the other hand, was an unknown quantity. And that alone made it dangerous.

"I am aware of that, Mr. O'Bannion. But you must stop her just the same."

"No disrespect intended, Princess, but why?"

"Because they are going to make another attempt on her life!" This time she didn't try to conceal the fear that had a grip on her throat. "In Philadelphia. And Mr. O'Bannion, I'm terrified that this time they'll succeed."

She'd definitely captured his interest. Caine took a pad of paper from the desk drawer, a silver pen from his pocket. "Okay," he said in a calm, authoritative voice, "why don't you calm down and start at the beginning."

# 6

"So TELL ME, Princess," Caine said, "what makes you believe your sister's in danger?"

"If she weren't in danger," Noel Giraudeau replied calmly over the long-distance telephone lines, "you wouldn't be sleeping in the next room. By the way, Mr. O'Bannion, do you carry a gun?"

Caine wondered if she was one of those people who thought that the bad guys obediently put down their weapons the moment you flashed your ID. "It goes with the territory, Princess. Now about your sister—"

"Have you ever had to shoot anyone with that gun?"

"Princess—"

"Noel," she reminded him. "And I'd really like to know, Mr. O'Bannion."

If he'd had any questions about this woman's identity in the beginning, Caine no longer harbored a single doubt. Her tone of voice was vastly familiar—her quiet self-assurance brooked no argument. It was an order. Softly spoken but couched in stone. Deciding that he'd only draw the conversation out longer by refusing to answer, Caine considered that if one princess was proving troublesome, two were a royal pain in the neck.

"The maniac who tried to kill the president didn't walk away."

There was a short, significant silence as Noel considered his words. "Good," she said finally. "I'm glad to know that you've been tested." Her tone became grave. "Because someone may die before all this is over, Mr. O'Bannion. And I don't want it to be my sister."

"If you want me to protect her, perhaps you'd better fill me in on what you know," he suggested with more patience than he was currently feeling.

"Of course. But first, what do you know about my grandfather?"

"Not a thing."

"I thought not. The summer of his twenty-first year, Phillipe Giraudeau, my grandfather, went on holiday in Arles after his graduation from Cambridge. The trip was a gift from his father."

"I see," Caine murmured, wondering just how long this little family saga was going to drag on.

"It was during this holiday that he fell instantly and passionately in love with a Gypsy flamenco dancer. Unfortunately, his father, Prince Leon, did not feel a flamenco dancer was an appropriate wife for the future regent of Montacroix."

"I suppose that's not so surprising."

"I suppose not," Noel agreed. "What my great-grandfather hadn't counted on was Phillipe marrying Katia in Spain without his blessing. Great-grandfather Leon was furious. He threatened to disinherit Phillipe."

It crossed Caine's mind that Phillipe may have been the first Giraudeau to have taken what his family considered a highly unsuitable bride, but as Chantal's own father had proved, he was not to be the last.

"Which, of course, he couldn't do because of the male line of ascendancy," he said.

"That's right. So you have studied our country's history, after all."

"A bit. And as delightful a love story as this is, Noel, I still can't see what it has to do with Chantal."

"I'm getting to that," she replied with equanimity. "Of course, once my father was born, Great-grandfather Leon welcomed the young couple back with open arms. So Montacroix's future was assured and Leon stepped down, allowing Phillipe to take his rightful place on the throne, an act that caused not a little dissension."

"Oh?"

"You see, my Grandmother Katia had been born with the gift of second sight. This caused some of her detractors to accuse her of being a witch. Her husband and children, however, learned to trust in her uncanny intuition."

Comprehension slowly dawned. "Intuition that has been passed down to her granddaughter."

"The president assured my father that you were very bright, Mr. O'Bannion. I do hope that you also believe— even a little—in clairvoyance." Her tone rose a little at the end, turning her softly spoken statement into a question.

Although he would be the last person to describe himself as a fanciful man, through the years certain inexplicable incidents had led Caine to believe that there were forces in the universe that science had not yet begun to explain.

Like the woman who walked into the Washington, D.C., police station five years ago claiming to have information concerning the kidnapping of a prominent British diplomat's two-year-old boy. The case had driven the cops crazy for years; there'd been no clues and every lead they had managed to uncover had resulted in yet another dead end.

Yet Margaret Reed, who'd only moved to the city a month prior to her visit to the department, and who alleged never to have heard about the kidnapping had described the child in startlingly accurate detail. She'd also given them a description of the kidnapper—a former pediatrics nurse at D.C. General Hospital—and an address of a red brick house where they could be found.

The woman was unable to name the city, and it seemed that every city and town in America possessed an Oak Street, so it took a while to locate the house. But five days later, Phoenix police, responding to a request from the Washington department, called to say they'd found the now seven-year-old child watching television inside a red brick house that was identical in every way to the one Mrs. Reed had described.

If that hadn't made Caine a believer, his own experience would have. In the predawn hours of the day of the assassination attempt against the president, he'd awakened in a cold sweat, a nightmare still reverberating in his head. The face of the man holding the gun was still vivid in his mind's eye as he reported for work. And later, when he saw that same unforgettable face in the crowd lining the sidewalk outside the hotel where the president was to speak, Caine didn't hesitate to push the president out of the way even as he pulled his own revolver. As he lay in Walter Reed hospital, waiting impatiently for his wound to heal, Caine realized that his early-morning dream had prevented the country from suffering a horribly painful tragedy.

"I like to think of myself as open-minded," he answered finally.

"You've no idea how happy I am to hear that," she said. "I had a dream last night, Mr. O'Bannion. A dream about Chantal. She was lying in the dark, surrounded by clouds of thick, dark smoke. I could hear her calling out to me, and I tried to save her, but a wall of flames kept me from reaching her."

Her words, spoken with a quiet intensity, had the effect of making the hair on his arms stand on end. "How do you know it was Philadelphia?"

"Because, over her cries and the roar of the flames, I could hear a bell tolling. That's how I found her in the first place, you see, by following the sound of the bell."

"The Liberty Bell."

"I saw it, famous crack and all." This time her softly modulated voice trembled a bit at the edges. "Chantal must not go to Philadelphia, Mr. O'Bannion. You must stop her."

Once again Caine considered exactly how difficult it was to talk Chantal out of anything. "I'll do my best."

Her relief was evident. "Thank you, Mr. O'Bannion. We all are very grateful to you."

As he replaced the receiver on its cradle, it crossed Caine's mind that the family would have a lot more to be thankful for if Chantal returned safe and sound to Montacroix eleven days from now.

Reminding himself that he had a busy day ahead, he attempted to get some sleep, but instead he kept staring at the ceiling, seeing Chantal's exquisite face, surrounded by flames, in the plaster swirls overhead.

CHANTAL HAD ALWAYS slept well in hotel rooms. This trip, however, was proving different. She tossed and turned, finding sleep to be elusive as the past ten days with Caine kept running through her mind over and over, like scenes from an all-night movie.

She couldn't stop thinking about him. At first light, during their early-morning runs, she'd noticed how their strides were so perfectly matched and couldn't help wondering if everything between them would be such a close and perfect fit.

During the long and wearying days, as she extolled the genius of the various artists represented in the exhibit, she'd make the mistake of glancing across the room and her gaze would collide with his—steady and watchful. Invariably, their eyes would hold, and in that suspended moment there would be a flash of heat so brilliant, so warm, that she was amazed they hadn't set the museum on fire from spontaneous combustion.

After that initial argument over where she would be eating her evening meal, he'd done his best to guide her to some wonderfully authentic ethnic restaurants, but although she was certain that the food was every bit as delicious as promised, she hadn't tasted a bite. All her attention had been riveted on Caine, on the smallest of details, like the lines fanning outward from his eyes, or the cleft splitting his chin, or the way his long, dark fingers curved around the handle of his coffee cup.

Afterward, driving back to the hotel in the limousine, Chantal would sit beside him, drinking in a dark, masculine scent that owed nothing to shaving lotions or expensive colognes but was his alone, and wonder what his lips would taste like on hers. How those strong, capable hands would feel on her body. . . .

Damn, she thought, sitting up to punch the plump goose-down pillow into a more acceptable shape, he had no right to take over her mind this way. She still couldn't believe the rash way she'd thrown herself at the man. Now that the seductive moment had passed, Chantal could admit to being grateful that he'd rejected her. Making love with Caine would have created problems she was not prepared to deal with.

If it had merely been a physical attraction, Chantal would have had no trouble handling it; she had, after all, been practicing self-denial for most of her life without any great difficulty. She'd simply thrown her passions into her work, experimenting with new styles, new textures, playing with pen and ink, chalk, flirting with misty, dreamy watercolors for a time before finally returning to her first love—oils.

Before coming to America, her mind had been filled with new ideas, and had it not been for this tour, she probably would have locked herself in her studio, working feverishly around the clock, ignoring her family's insistence that she stop to eat, until all her visions were safely captured on canvas. That was the way she worked. Unrepentantly impulsive, she'd always painted in mad dashes as inspiration struck.

Logical Burke, on the other hand, would mull over a problem for as long as it took, looking at all sides before acting. And Noel, despite her amazing gift of clairvoyance and her romantic streak, was as practical and unfrivolous as a Montacroix farm wife.

The truth was, Caine O'Bannion frightened Chantal. If she wasn't careful, she knew, she could fall head over heels in love with him. And that, she reminded herself, picking up her sketch pad as she abandoned trying to sleep, was not something she would permit to happen.

Ten minutes later, she was putting the final touches on a sketch of the man she could not get out of her mind.

IN A RENTED ROOM directly across from the hotel, Chantal's would-be assassins were forced to bide their time, as they had been doing since her arrival in the country twelve days earlier.

"This waiting is beginning to get on my nerves," the bearded man complained.

The other man looked up from his crossword puzzle. "Patience, Karl." He frowned as he tried to think of an eight-letter word for revenge. "By this time tomorrow, our mission will be accomplished."

"What makes you think we can pry her loose from O'Bannion?"

"By changing her plans at the last minute and deciding to stay with her friend in Philadelphia, the princess has taken care of that little matter for us. . . . Of course! Vendetta." He smiled as he filled in the blanks.

Satisfied, he rose from the table, poured some schnapps into a pair of glasses and handed one to the man whose gaze was directed at Chantal's darkened window. "To Philadelphia," he said, raising his glass in a toast.

"To Philadelphia."

AFTER A SLEEPLESS NIGHT, and his early-morning run with the princess, Caine sat in the coffee shop of the hotel, drinking a five-dollar cup of coffee and plotting strategy with Drew Tremayne.

"You sound as if you're taking the sister's premonition seriously," Drew said, plucking a fresh cinnamon roll from the silver basket between them.

There weren't many men in whom Caine would have confided his fears. After having worked with Drew for six years, he was one of a select few. Caine would trust his friend with his life, as indeed he did every time they went on an assignment together.

"I can't afford not to," he said, cringing as Drew stirred a second spoonful of sugar into his coffee, tasted, then added one more for good measure. "I'm amazed you have any teeth left."

"Never had a cavity. According to my daddy, all us Tremaynes are born with strong teeth and bones, quick minds and incredible good looks."

"Don't forget modesty."

He grinned. "That, too," he said, digging into a bowl of cereal.

"I can't believe I actually know someone who eats colored cereal with miniature marshmallows for breakfast."

"Beats the hell out of those nuts and twigs you eat."

"You and the princess would get along great."

"Think so?"

"Yeah, she never met a food she didn't like, either."

"You know," Drew murmured, "I'm really beginning to like that lady." He licked the bun's white frosting off his fingers. "Are you going to eat that blueberry muffin?"

"The two of you are definitely a match made in heaven," Caine muttered, pushing the basket across the table. "Think of all the gooey pastries you could get the royal baker to whip up."

"The idea is sounding better and better," Drew said, plucking the muffin from its bed of white damask. "Unfortunately, I'm afraid I'd strike out before I even got up to bat. The lady is far too busy mooning over you to even notice me."

"That's ridiculous."

Drew stopped in the act of buttering the fragrant, hot muffin. "What is it about Chantal that bothers you, Caine? The fact that she's ridiculously rich or breathtakingly beautiful? And, besides being sexy as hell, is genuinely nice?"

It was certainly not the first time he and Drew had discussed the opposite sex. As a matter of fact, women usually finished in the top three categories of conversation, right up there with work and the Redskins. But something about Chantal—about his reaction to her—had Caine feeling strangely unsettled.

"What bothers me is the fact that she's the most intransigent, impossible woman I've ever met. And much as I'd love to stay here and watch you create havoc with your cholesterol, I'd better get upstairs before she takes it into her fool head to leave without me," Caine grumbled as he stood up.

"She's a mite headstrong, all right," Drew agreed easily with a slow drawl that was the result of seven generations of Tennessee ancestors. "But some men prefer a challenge." Repressed laughter glinted in his eyes as he looked at Caine. "Seems to me I remember you being one of those men."

"The princess is a helluva lot more than a challenge," Caine growled as he signed the check. "She's an ulcer just waiting to happen."

"You could always 'fess up. Hell, Caine, she's an intelligent lady. If she heard all the facts, she just might be a little more cooperative."

"There's nothing I'd love better than to drop all this damn pretense. Unfortunately, that decision isn't mine to make."

"So, I guess all we can do for the time being is stick close and wait for this guy, whoever he is, to make his move. You realize, of course, that when she does find out how we've lied to her, the princess is going to be madder than a wet hen."

Drew wasn't saying anything Caine hadn't already considered. It had crossed his mind more than once that when Chantal did ultimately discover his deception, she wouldn't want anything further to do with him.

As unappealing as that idea was, Caine didn't dwell on it. For now, all his thoughts had to be directed toward keeping her safe. But as he left the restaurant, he realized that sometime between their initial clash at the airport and last night's heated kiss, he had crossed the line between professionalism and his escalating obsession for a woman who was light-years beyond his reach.

# 7

THE PHILADELPHIA MUSEUM OF ART crowned Fairmont Hill like a massive, resplendent, misplaced Greco-Roman temple. Although it wasn't as dazzling as Washington's National Gallery of Art, Chantal felt that the facade of the beautifully proportioned building seemed to promise something extraordinarily wonderful waiting within. A promise the museum definitely lived up to, she discovered.

She spent the better part of her first day in the city with the curator on the second floor of the museum, supervising the final touches on the exhibit. If she was at all intimidated by the idea of her works being hung in close proximity to works by Poussin, Rubens, or Cézanne, Chantal did not dwell on it. For too many years she'd puttered around at her art, longing to work up the nerve to paint seriously but always afraid that she'd never produce anything that came close to the art of Picasso. Or Matisse. Or any of the other artists who'd come before her.

Finally, it had been her mother's statement about how she'd had to learn not to compare herself with other performers—everyone had a unique gift to offer—that finally gave Chantal the courage to try. Although that had been only five years ago, it seemed she could not remember a life without her art. Heaven knew, it had certainly gotten her through some tough times these past couple of years.

She was relieved at how fast the work on the exhibit progressed. The paintings, having been sent on ahead, had arrived the day before, and fortunately, the museum employees were well prepared; each of the accompanying white cardboard cards had been printed with careful accuracy, the walls had been painted a soft ivory in order to better display the paintings, and complementary lighting had been installed. Although she'd never considered herself a superstitious woman, Chantal decided to take the fact that everything was turning out to be absolutely, amazingly perfect as a propitious omen.

"Can you believe how smoothly everything went?" she exclaimed happily to Caine as they walked back out to the waiting car.

When she had first expressed surprise that they would be having the same driver throughout the tour, Caine had mumbled some vague explanation about security clearances. Although she hadn't really understood, she rather liked the idea of Drew Tremayne traveling with them. Not only was his presence making it more difficult for her to succumb to temptation with Caine, she was beginning to genuinely like the man.

Although he probably hadn't said more than a dozen words to her, there were times, especially when she and Caine were arguing about something, that Chantal would glance up into the rearview mirror and see Drew smiling back at her. His easy, good-natured grin did wonders to soothe her temper whenever Caine began behaving like an ogre, which seemed to happen every time she decided to scrap the carefully planned itinerary and take off somewhere on the spur of the moment. Spontaneity, she had decided, was definitely not Caine O'Bannion's strong suit.

"It wasn't as bad as I expected it to be," Caine admitted gruffly. His eyes, ever alert behind his dark glasses, scanned the grounds, looking for . . . what? he wondered.

He'd been distant all day. Chantal found herself missing his dry humor and reluctant smiles, even the way he had of issuing orders like some Far Eastern potentate. She couldn't help wondering if his behavior was due to what had happened between them last night, but not wanting to reopen such a potentially dangerous subject, she opted not to push.

The view from the top of the hill was breathtaking. Chantal paused, looking out over the broad sweep of Benjamin Franklin Parkway as it disappeared into the lush greenery of Fairmount Park. Sunset gilded the serpentine Schuylkill River as scullers' oars cut smoothly through its waters; in the distance she could see the Victorian wedding-cake facade of City Hall. Flat-roofed row houses spread outward in crisp geometric formation for miles and miles.

"I wish we had time to visit the park," she murmured, her gaze drifting over the acres of trees that were wearing their bright spring coats of kelly green. Pink and white hyacinths, sunshine-yellow daffodils and azaleas added enticing splashes of color. "I'd give anything to kick my shoes off and run across all that grass."

"That doesn't sound like very royal behavior to me."

"Perhaps not." If he was trying to annoy her, he was right on target, but Chantal was feeling too good to respond in kind. "But it certainly sounds like fun." Exhaling a slight sigh, she glanced down at her watch and continued walking toward the car. "I suppose we'd better be going."

"We should if you want to change clothes before your friend's dinner party," Caine agreed. "Speaking of which—"

"I'm not going to give in on this one, Caine," Chantal insisted, holding up her hand to stop his protest. "There is no reason why I should stay at a hotel when Blair Sherwood has a perfectly fine guest room. She was my best friend during our boarding school days together in Lucerne. We haven't seen each other for years. We'll probably be up all night talking."

Caine had several very good reasons why she should be staying at a hotel instead of this old girlfriend's house. And every one of them had to do with Chantal's safety. All day long he'd been tempted just to tell her the truth—everything, beginning with the president's request that he protect her to her sister's late-night phone call. Unfortunately, an order was an order. He wondered if the president realized just how badly he'd tied Caine's hands.

"People change," he said, opening the car door for her.

"Now there's a pithy phrase. Remind me to write that one down." The smile she gave him as she slid across the seat took the edge off her words.

"What I was trying to point out," he continued, "was that perhaps you and this Sherwood woman won't have anything in common any longer. Perhaps you'll run out of things to talk about before you finish the soup course. Worse yet, maybe you'll hate each other. Or there's always the possibility that she'll be so jealous of your position she'll make your visit miserable."

"I believe I'll risk it."

"You are a princess, don't forget."

Chantal reminded herself that temper took more energy than she was prepared to summon right now. "How could I? When you are so kind as to keep pointing it out."

There was a sound somewhere between a cough and a laugh from the front seat. When Chantal met Drew's eyes in the rearview mirror, he flashed her yet another of his encouraging grins. "Besides, I was also a princess years ago, and it certainly didn't get in the way of our friendship then."

"People change."

"So you said."

Having reached a stalemate, both fell silent as the limousine inched along in the rush-hour traffic on the parkway. Chantal wondered once again what it was that had Caine so cross.

Caine knew he'd been behaving abominably. He also knew that Chantal was puzzled by what she perceived to be his gruff, inattentive attitude. How could he explain that all his senses were on red alert, watching for something, anything that might harm her? He'd actually begun to wonder if clairvoyance were contagious.

"I still don't know why you had to change your plans at the last minute," he said for what had to be the umpteenth time that day. "Why can't you get your girl talk over with, then return to the hotel?"

"And have Drew stay up all night waiting for my call?"

"It's his job."

"Whatever you may think of pampered royalty, my parents taught me to be considerate of others."

Caine wondered what Chantal would say if she knew that instead of making Drew's life easier, she was complicating it. Because unless he could get her to change her mind before dinner was over, he and Drew were going to be spending the night parked across the street from the Sherwood house. Caine could only hope that such surveillance would be enough to prevent Noel's unsettling dream from becoming a reality.

CAINE DECIDED that Blair Sherwood's gray stone Germantown mansion was a tribute to both great wealth and even greater taste. The facade of the house was actually rather plain, befitting the simplicity endorsed by its original Quaker owners. But once inside, a visitor was greeted by a vast checkerboard floor of Valley Forge marble leading to a gracefully curving stairway.

Blair Sherwood was an attractive, self-assured young matron who, as Chantal had predicted, appeared not a whit intimidated by the idea of having a princess as a houseguest. After greeting Chantal with a hug, she proceeded to lead them on a grand tour of the recently refurbished house, chatting gaily as she pointed out the hundreds of authentic colonial implements.

"It took David three years to collect those pipes," she said, pointing out the inlaid Federal pipe rack filled with long clay meerschaums. "We spent every weekend cruising the antique shops and flea markets."

"Flea markets?" Chantal asked with amusement. She couldn't picture the teenage girl who'd arrived at school with an entire closet of haute couture haggling over prices at a flea market.

"I know, I know," Blair agreed on a throaty laugh. "This from the girl who was always afraid of chipping her manicure. But really, Chantal, Philadelphia is just one big attic filled with heirlooms. You've no idea the treasures you can find in a flea market."

She pointed out an intricate chessboard stand, hinged so it could fit against the wall. "I bought that from a young couple who had inherited her grandmother's home and were cleaning out the basement. You'd never believe what I paid for it."

Her smile reminded Caine of the cat who'd just dined on a particularly succulent canary. All that was missing were the bright yellow feathers sticking out of her mouth. "It was such a steal we made a deal for everything they had. David rented a truck and we came home with enough castoffs to finish the library and the dining room."

"You and David have made a wonderful home," Chantal murmured as she ran her fingers over the design of a delftware bowl filled with fresh flowers.

She couldn't help wondering what it would be like to spend weekends with the man you loved searching for those unique little things that somehow managed to make a house a home. Greg hadn't wanted a home of their own; whenever she'd broached the subject, he'd insisted that his Grand Prix racing schedule made buying a house a ridiculous waste of time. She found it difficult to believe, looking at her schoolgirl friend, that Blair was now the mother of three children—a pair of six-year-old twin daughters and a three-month-old baby boy.

Chantal had been surprised by the stab of envy she'd felt upon seeing Blair's children. Greg hadn't wanted children. A fact he'd made painfully clear after she'd excitedly announced her pregnancy two months after their wedding. When she'd miscarried four months later, her husband had not bothered to hide his relief.

"Lord knows it's been a chore," Blair said on a long-suffering sigh that Chantal knew was feigned. "And the upstairs still needs a lot of work. In fact, the reason I didn't ask you to stay sooner was that I wasn't certain we'd be able to get at least one guest room finished in time."

She glanced over at Caine. "I'm sorry that I can't invite you to stay here as well, Mr. O'Bannion, but I'd never relegate a guest to sleeping in a room filled with cans of paint and turpentine, not to mention all the sawdust and rolls of wallpaper."

"I wouldn't mind," Caine immediately assured her.

"Nonsense. You'll be much more comfortable at the hotel," she insisted. "But I do insist that you come back for dinner tonight."

"It must be exciting," Chantal said. "Working on such a long-term project."

"'Long-term' is the definitive description," Blair said. "But now that it's finally beginning to come together, I think it's been worthwhile. And of course Karen and Kathy adore living in such a rambling old place. With all the hidden rooms and secret passages, it's tailor-made for playing hide-and-seek."

Karen and Kathy were the twins. They were attractive, polite and, Blair had assured Chantal, exceedingly bright. Nearly perfect, if you could overlook their penchant for pets. The house currently boasted six cats, five being newly born kittens for whom Blair, displaying her usual brisk efficiency, had already located homes.

"Secret passages?" Caine asked, instantly alert.

"This house was built by Quakers," Blair explained. "It was one of the stops on the Underground Railroad during the Civil War. Consequently, there are several hidden hallways behind the walls. They are so cleverly secreted that we were in the house six months before we discovered them all. Later we learned that the blueprints of the house were on file at the historical society."

As she proceeded to relate an amusing story about discovering the twins hiding in the whispering closet adjoining the parlor, eavesdropping on their parents' late-night conversations, Caine considered the added risks involved in Chantal spending the night in a house riddled with secret passages.

"In fact," Blair finished on a lilt of laughter, "Stormy had her kittens in the wall behind our bedroom. We hadn't even known she was pregnant until we heard mewings behind our headboard."

Chantal shared in the laughter, noticing that Caine was frowning as he looked around the room. His hands were shoved into his pockets, but she could tell that he was clenching and unclenching his fists. "Caine?"

He realized that both women were looking at him with interest. "Sorry," he said, "I was thinking of something."

"You must forgive me, Mr. O'Bannion," Blair said, "for chattering away when you must have better things to do than listen to my silly domestic dramas."

She linked her hand through his arm, leading him out of the book-paneled library toward the foyer. "Chantal and I have so much to talk about, and all of it would undoubtedly bore you to tears. So, I'll let you get back to your hotel. You will come to dinner, won't you? I promise that it will be an interesting crowd. And something you might especially enjoy for a change—there won't be a single politician in the bunch."

As he allowed himself to be directed toward the front door, Caine decided that the woman was a velvet bulldozer. Less direct than Chantal, perhaps, but every bit as tenacious when it came to getting her own way. If she wanted Chantal to spend the night in her home and Chantal wanted to stay there as well, Caine didn't know how he was going to change either woman's mind. Not and keep his promise to the president.

"Of course I'll come," he said. "Thank you for inviting me."

"Well, goodness, it's not that often that we have both a princess and an under secretary of state as dinner guests."

"Deputy under secretary."

She patted his arm reassuringly. "Don't worry. If you're half as efficient as Chantal claims, you'll undoubtedly be earning a promotion any day."

Mumbling something that could have been a vague agreement or a farewell, Caine left the house, feeling uncomfortably impotent when the bulbous Georgian door closed behind him.

"ALL RIGHT," Blair said, turning to Chantal once they were alone, "let's go upstairs. You can tell me all about the hunk while you're unpacking."

"'The hunk'?" Chantal asked, surprised to discover yet another Americanism she was not familiar with.

"That sexy diplomat who just left. The one who can't take his eyes off you."

"Oh, Caine." Chantal smiled. Hunk. It suited him, she decided. "He's been assigned to make the tour run more smoothly and, I suspect, to keep the outrageous, jet-setting princess from embarrassing either her own country or the United States."

"You are much more than an assignment, darling. The way those magnificent gray eyes were eating you up, if you'd been a chocolate bar, you'd have been a goner."

As her friend's words hit a little too close to home, Chantal felt color flood into her cheeks. "Which reminds me, I'd like to visit Hershey before leaving Pennsylvania." Chantal found the idea of a whole town fixated on chocolate absolutely irresistible.

"Don't try to change the subject," Blair said as they climbed the curving stairway to the second floor. "Here we are," she said brightly, circumventing a trio of five-gallon paint cans stacked up in the narrow hallway as she opened the door to the most ornately decorated of the bedrooms. "The Princess Suite, as David has dubbed it."

As she entered the decorus but inviting room, Chantal felt a pang of something indiscernible. Not envy, not jealousy, but something else. Regret for her own lost opportunities? Perhaps.

"It's lovely," she murmured, going over to the Palladian windows and looking out at the backyard gardens, where daffodils and tulips vied for the most colorful, while lush green ivy climbed the stone walls of the house. A lilac bush was in bloom beside a gazebo, its flowers a riotous display of brilliant purple. A slate roof slanted down over a flagstone terrace. "And your view is wonderful."

"David brought those garden seats home from an auction last month," Blair said, pointing out the Oriental seats that resembled brightly painted ceramic drums. "To tell the truth, they're a little gaudy for my taste, but it was obvious that he was in love with them, so I decided, what the hell." She smiled. "I think they're beginning to grow on me. The past couple of weeks I've found I can actually look at them without cringing."

"You must love David a great deal," Chantal murmured. Although she'd only met him twice, the first time at Blair's wedding, then once again at her own, she remembered a tall, lanky man with a receding hairline and gentle eyes reminiscent of an Amish farmer.

"I adore him. Some more days than others, but there's not a day that goes by that I don't thank my lucky stars that I broke my leg on that miserable Swiss ski run just as David was schussing by."

"That's nice," Chantal murmured. "Not that you broke your leg, of course, but that you're still in love. After all these years."

"That's what love is all about."

"Is it?" Chantal sank down onto the four-poster. "I thought I was in love with Greg."

"That was infatuation."

Of course it was, Chantal agreed silently. With the twenty-twenty vision of hindsight, she could see that now. But how did one know when it was happening? "How did you know that your feelings for David were the real thing, and not infatuation?" she asked softly, tracing the pattern on the star-of-Bethlehem quilt with her fingernail.

"I suppose it helped that he saw me at my worst," Blair said thoughtfully. "Whining and crying and acting like a real ninny. And even that didn't turn him off."

Chantal compared that with Greg, who, after his initial relief, had found her miscarriage so distasteful that he'd taken off for a gambling holiday in Monaco with his friends. "So, the trick is to break a leg?"

"Or come down with the flu. If a man can survive the galloping crud, he'll stick around for anything. Even morning sickness." The laughter faded from Blair's eyes as she saw that Chantal was deadly serious. "Caine O'Bannion looks like a sticker," she offered. "Probably make a good husband...for a woman looking to get married."

"Well, that's definitely not me."

"Pooh, don't be ridiculous. All women, whether they admit it or not, want to get married."

"Now who's being ridiculous?" Shaking her head with good-natured frustration, Chantal stood up and began unpacking her suitcase. "I happen to know several women who are single and quite content. They lead active, varied social lives, have interesting careers and manage to succeed very well without a live-in man."

"All right, point taken," Blair reluctantly agreed. "But we weren't talking about those women. We were talking about you."

"I've been married," Chantal reminded her friend as she put her lingerie away in a scented, lined drawer of the mahogany serpentine chest.

"You were married to the wrong man, so it doesn't count."

"Of course it counts."

"Not really. You weren't even married in the church."

"Mama and Papa wouldn't allow it. They were certain it wouldn't work." Chantal opened the closet. All the hangers were covered with plump, scented quilting. How she wished she had even the teeniest bit of Blair's extraordinary flair for detail. "Unfortunately, they were right."

"So, since the church doesn't consider that you were married, you must not have been," Blair continued to argue. "Or have you become so stubborn you're willing to argue with the Pope?"

"I certainly wouldn't be the first woman to try," Chantal murmured. "Besides, church wedding or not, the divorce still hurt, Blair. A lot."

Although Chantal's back was turned as she hung up her clothing, it would have been impossible to miss the pain in her voice. "Of course it did, honey," Blair answered quickly. "Hey," she said, seeming to change the subject, "did I mention that I saw you on television in the last Olympics? I thought for sure that you were going to sweep the course."

"So did I, until that damn water hazard. Unfortunately, landing unceremoniously on your derriere in the middle of a pond doesn't win you a medal."

Blair was busily lining up Chantal's crystal perfume bottles atop a Queen Anne dresser. "I thought you landed with a certain élan. But as unhappy as I was for you, do you know what I was thinking?"

"What?"

"About that time in Lucerne, when we were both taking those damn dressage lessons and you flew over the top of your horse when he came to that sudden stop in front of the brick wall. Remember?"

"How could I forget? I was in bed for a week with a concussion." Chantal turned, brushing her hair off her forehead. "I still have the scar."

Blair lifted the frosted-glass lid of one amethyst-hued bottle and took an appreciative sniff. The scent was expensive and obviously uniquely blended for its wearer. "Then you also undoubtedly recall that the first day the doctor let you out of bed, you went right back out and rode the course again. Perfectly."

Chantal got Blair's point. Loud and clear. "Getting back on a horse is a great deal different from getting remarried."

"Is it?" Glancing at her watch, Blair put down the perfume bottle and turned to leave the room. "I've got to go before Jason begins screaming for his dinner," she said. "But do me a favor and think about what I've said. You're too young to be so jaded, darling."

"I'm not at all jaded," Chantal said with astonishment.

"Aren't you? What do *you* call a twenty-nine-year-old woman who's sworn off marriage?"

"I didn't exactly say I've sworn off it. I only said I'm not ready to think about remarrying anyone."

Blair looked unconvinced. "Relationships are difficult enough without setting up artificial barriers."

How strange to hear her own words to Caine tossed back in her face. "You don't have to tell me that they're difficult. That's one of the reasons I'm not ready for any kind of relationship right now."

"How about an affair? Do you think you could handle that?"

Chantal thought about Caine. About the way she felt when he looked at her. About the way his gaze could melt the ice she hadn't even been aware had grown inside her. "I don't know," she murmured. "I'll think about it."

"You do that," Blair said, nodding her satisfaction. From the other side of the house both women heard the strident demands of the Sherwood family's youngest. "I've got to go play mommy," Blair said. "Why don't you take a long bubble bath before dinner?"

"That sounds heavenly."

"Good." Impulsively, Blair reached out and threw her arms around Chantal. "I'm so happy to see you."

As she returned the hug, Chantal caught the faint scent of milk emanating from Blair's skin and decided that the warm, sweet fragrance moved her more than any of the expensive perfumes currently laying claim to the top of the dresser.

"Not nearly as happy as I am to see you," she answered truthfully. The years between them fell away, and for a brief, shining moment, Chantal felt like the laughing, carefree, oh-so-naive girl she'd once been.

# 8

THE PHILADELPHIANS SELECTED for the honor of meeting Princess Chantal Giraudeau de Montacroix were unmistakably Main Line. As he diligently worked his way through the ambitiously French dinner, Caine had difficulty deciding which backs were straighter—those belonging to the chairs or the guests. They were not the type of people normally considered potential murderers, but experience had taught Caine that he could take nothing for granted.

Over a superb terrine of duck with Armagnac and green peppercorns, he exchanged a few words with a stiff-necked dermatologist whose unique solution to the city's homeless problem was to simply give the people bus tickets to Florida.

"It's warmer there," the physician explained earnestly. "They'll be able to camp out on the beaches for free."

Several replies raced through Caine's mind, each more caustic than the last. Deciding that nothing would be gained by embarrassing either Chantal, Blair, who he'd determined was a nice woman, or David Sherwood, whose devotion to his wife was obvious, Caine mumbled something into his glass as he took a long swallow of wine. All the while he kept a surreptitious eye on Chantal, every muscle in his body tensed, prepared for immediate action.

At the head of the table, seated in the place of honor, the princess was engaged in what appeared to be a stimulating conversation with the man on her right—an elderly, balding professor emeritus of the University of Pennsylvania. Knowing that she'd undoubtedly appear just as fascinated listening to the drivel the dermatologist was spouting, Caine found himself once again impressed by her chameleonlike ability to adapt instantly to her surroundings.

She'd chosen a plum silk evening suit, the deep neckline of the beaded jacket allowing an enticing glimpse of the top of her breasts. At first Caine considered that her perfumed flesh gleaming in the candlelight reminded him of marble, but he quickly corrected himself. Marble was too cold. Too hard. Amethysts glowed warmly at her earlobes; hammered gold gleamed at her wrists. Her hands fluttered as she talked, like small birds; her slender fingers were unadorned, save for that ever-present silver ring.

He was enjoying watching her when he suddenly felt a hand on his thigh. Caine immediately turned his attention to the sleek blond woman seated beside him. "You're certainly quiet," she said.

"I was enjoying the meal. Mrs. Sherwood certainly has a knack for planning a menu, doesn't she?" he asked politely, seeking an impersonal opening gambit.

"Blair attended the École de Cuisine la Varenne in Paris," replied the woman, who'd been introduced earlier as Elizabeth Bancroft. Cutting into a small bacon-and-onion tart with her right hand, she scored an enticing trail up his leg beneath the snowy damask tablecloth with her left.

"But that's our Blair," Elizabeth continued, "always working at self-improvement. At least this is better than the Japanese cooking course she took last year. As much as I absolutely adore Blair, I simply had to draw the line at raw fish. And let me tell you, I wasn't alone."

"You sound as if you know her well," Caine managed as the server took away his plate and replaced it with the next course. As the treacherous hand inched upward, he vowed to stop it before it reached its destination. The only problem was, he wasn't certain that Chantal would approve of him dumping the thin slices of salmon wrapped around a sybaritic filling of onions, cream and salmon roe into the woman's Dior-clad lap.

When the bearded blond waiter—clad in the requisite black tie—appeared beside Elizabeth, the hand abandoned its quest, causing Caine to breathe a deep sigh of relief. "We're close friends. In fact, she's been a guest at my last three weddings."

"Really?" If Caine had needed additional proof that this lady was perhaps not as stiffly Main Line as the other guests, the reference to her multiple marriages was it.

"I didn't know her the first two times," Elizabeth explained casually. "So tell me, Mr. O'Bannion, what do you think of our fair city?"

The hand was back. The muscles of his leg clenched under her exploring touch. "I've always enjoyed Philadelphia."

"Oh?" The politely interested expression on her face belied the fact that her fingers beneath the tablecloth were becoming dangerously intimate. "Are you from New England?"

"My mother's family lives in Boston. I spent most of my childhood there." Deciding he had nothing to lose, Caine covered the hand with his own and gently returned it to Elizabeth Bancroft's lap. Her expression didn't alter.

"Lovely city, Boston," she agreed with a brief nod. "Although it does have a tendency to blow its own horn a bit, don't you think?" Her smile was ever so slightly condescending. "We Philadelphians prefer to think of our city as one of the best-kept secrets in the world."

Caine was more than a little relieved when for the remainder of the meal the conversation consisted of a treatise on Philadelphia's illustrious past. Over medallions of lamb on a bed of parsley served with truffles and Madeira cream sauce, buttered scallions and accompanied by a watercress, tomato and basil salad, Elizabeth lectured Caine practically nonstop. Although he hoped that he managed to appear at least moderately interested, he was aware of her words only on the most distant of levels as he watched the others watching Chantal.

"That's very interesting," he said when the waiter arrived once again to clear away their plates. At the opposite end of the long table, Blair was announcing that dessert would be served in the front parlor. "You have a remarkable knowledge of the area. If you're ever looking for work, you could probably get a job in the history department at Penn."

"But that's precisely what I do," she informed him as she took a sip of the robust ruby-red Pinot Noir wine. Beneath the cover of the tablecloth, the hand returned, more provocative than ever. "I'm a professor there. In fact, I received tenure last year." She gave him a smile loaded with feminine invitation. "And now that I've done my civic duty and filled you in on all our city has to offer, why don't we skip dessert and I'll take you on a more personal tour?"

"Look," he said quietly, for her ears only, "I'm flattered by your interest, really I am. But you see, I'm kind of spoken for."

"Oh really?" She arched a blond brow. "Are you engaged?"

"No, but—"

"Living with someone?"

"No."

A knowing smile quirked at the corners of her mouth. "Pinned? Going steady?"

"Not exactly." He was beginning to feel like a fool. Why the hell did he have to explain anything to a woman he'd met only an hour ago?

"Don't tell me you're gay."

"No, not that, either."

"Thank heavens," the woman breathed with relief. "That would have been a terrible waste."

"Excuse me," Chantal's familiar voice interrupted as she stopped beside his chair on the way out of the room. "I hate to interrupt what appears to be a fascinating conversation, but if you don't mind, Caine, I need to speak to you in the library. It's about tomorrow's exhibition."

Pushing the Chippendale chair back from the table, he rose instantly. "Don't worry about a thing. After all, it's my job to see that things run smoothly." He managed a look of feigned regret as he turned back toward Elizabeth. "Perhaps I'll see you later."

"Perhaps." Her gaze was shrewd as her eyes moved back and forth between Caine and Chantal. "Then again, perhaps not. At any rate, it was a pleasure meeting you, Mr. O'Bannion. And Princess, I do hope that your tour is a smashing success."

A strange tension lingered in the air. Unable to decode it, Chantal wished fleetingly that her sister were here. With her remarkable clairvoyance, Noel always proved adept at reading people's emotions. "Thank you."

"You're welcome. Oh, Mr. O'Bannion," Elizabeth called out as the pair began to leave the wainscoted dining room.

Caine half turned. "Yes?"

This time Elizabeth Bancroft's emerald eyes were dancing with undisguised humor. "Good luck."

WHILE CHANTEL PROCEEDED to charm the assembled gathering of Main Line Philadelphians, the dark-haired man sat alone in his luxurious suite on the twenty-fifth floor of the Palace Hotel, staring at a picture of the princess on her wedding day. Clad in a frothy confection of lace, satin and seed pearls, a tiara of diamonds perched atop her gleaming dark hair, she appeared to be a princess from a fairy tale. All that was missing were the glass slippers.

She was smiling into the camera lens, and as the man's eyes settled on those full, rosy lips, he was momentarily distracted to realize that he could recall their taste even now. Not only their taste, but their softness, as well. And the sweet scent of her hair, the petallike silkiness of her skin, the inviting, dark depths of her eyes. Such vivid memories came as a startling surprise after all this time.

Then again, perhaps such whispers from the past were not so unusual, he decided, rising from the chair to resume his pacing. After all, Chantal had always been a remarkably memorable woman. In a way, he almost regretted what he was about to do. She was so breathtakingly beautiful; how could any mere mortal destroy such exquisite perfection? But just as he began to vacillate, other more painful memories managed to make themselves heard in the heated turmoil of his mind, and a single truth stood out like a shining beacon.

The Princess Chantal Giraudeau de Montacroix must die.


"WHY DID THAT Bancroft woman wish you good luck?" Chantal asked as they entered the library.

Caine shrugged. "She was undoubtedly referring to the tour."

"I suppose that's why she was stripping you with her eyes all during dinner?"

Caine could feel the heat beginning to rise at the back of his neck. "Don't be ridiculous."

"She was," Chantal insisted. "Fortunately for you, it was obvious that you were resisting her feminine ploys."

"If she had made a pass at me, I certainly would have resisted," Caine hedged. "Now, what's the problem?" Wondering if she had seen something or someone that may have triggered some internal alarm, he was considering saying the hell with orders and admitting everything when her next words caught him off guard.

"I need you to tell me a joke."

"A what?"

"A joke. Please, Caine, I've just been through one of the more agonizingly boring meals of my life. I need a little levity if I'm to survive dessert."

"You looked as if you were having a great time."

"I have been taught to appear fascinated by the most inane conversations, and if I do say so myself, I perform my duty very well. Now, however, I need some assistance to get through the next hour."

Caine searched his mind, finding it a complete blank.

"Caine," Chantal protested, "I'm counting on you."

"I'm working on it. Just give me a minute, okay?" He remembered a story the guys at the gym had been laughing about the last time he'd worked out there. Not only was the joke inappropriate for mixed company, it was definitely not princess material. Suddenly he recalled a joke his eight-year-old nephew, Danny, had told him a few weeks ago.

"Okay. What's round and purple and conquered the world?"

Chantal was silent a moment as she considered his question. "I don't know," she said finally. "What is round and purple and conquered the world?"

"Alexander the Grape."

"That's a terrible joke."

"If it's so bad, why are you laughing?"

"I don't want to hurt your feelings. I am, after all, a very compassionate woman."

"Sorry, but I'm going to have to argue with you about that one, Princess."

"I don't know what you're talking about."

Unable to resist touching her another moment, Caine brushed his knuckles along her cheekbones. "Don't you?" His voice was rough with an unmistakable desire that thrilled her. "Are you saying that you don't realize that you've been driving me crazy? That all I can think about is you? How right you feel in my arms, the soft, sweet taste of your lips, the way a single look from you, or a mere touch, can make me feel as if I'm sinking into quicksand?" His lips skimmed the path his hands had warmed. "Dammit, what is it about you?"

Chantal tried to ignore the restless anger she heard in his tone, concentrating instead on his words. Words that so closely echoed her own tumultuous feelings. "I don't know," she whispered, "but whatever it is, I feel the same way about you."

Unable to resist the hidden appeal, Caine leaned closer, watching as Chantal's lips—those soft, incredible lips he'd tasted over and over again in his memory—trembled apart. It happened slowly. So slowly, so gradually, that either could have backed away. Chantal watched, fascinated as his mouth lowered to hers.

It was just as it had been the first time. His lips were gentle, persuasive, causing a stream of pure pleasure to flow through her. Meltingly soft and caressingly delicate, the kiss created a shimmering, hypnotizing cloud that settled over her mind.

After a long moment, he eased back. "You've no idea how much I've needed this." Caine framed her uplifted face with his hands, his thumbs brushing her cheeks.

"Yes, I do." Her arms wrapped possessively around him, the gesture fitting her body more closely to his. "Because I was going mad during dinner."

His hands moved against her back, palms tracing lazy circles up and down her spine, soothing gestures that excited rather than calmed. "Don't feel like the Lone Ranger," he muttered against her lips.

As she moved invitingly against him, her slender body was a contradiction of strength and delicacy that had him yearning to rip off her plum silk dinner suit and take her here, now, atop the burl walnut partner's desk Blair Sherwood had expressed such pride in. Lord, how he wanted her!

Chantal's breath shuddered out as he kissed her from one corner of her mouth to the other, which was almost Caine's undoing. For a man accustomed to maintaining control, he was finding what Chantal could do to both his mind and his body equally intriguing and disconcerting.

It was too easy to forget that she wasn't the woman for him when her lips were clinging so avidly to his. The feel of her softly yielding curves against his body drove all logic and intellect from his mind. Needs welled up inside of him, but even as his blood began to burn, Caine managed to ease her away.

"We'd better get back to the others before they send out a search party."

Chantal was breathless. She was trembling from desire, but something told her that merely making love to

Caine wouldn't be enough. She wanted more. She wanted . . . what? It was impossible to sort out her tumbled thoughts while her head was still spinning.

"I suppose that would be a good idea," she said. With hands that were not as steady as she would have liked, she reached into her beaded evening bag and pulled out a jeweled tube of lipstick and a slender gold compact.

"Wait." Caine's eyes didn't leave hers as he caught her hand, stopping the creamy plum lipstick on its way to her mouth. Although this time his kiss lasted no longer than a heartbeat, it was no less devastating. "If you were my woman," he said, tracing her softly parted lips with a fingertip, "you'd have to give up that stuff."

"Oh, really?" she said archly as she gathered her wits about her.

Now that he'd discovered the fires lurking beneath the frosty regal exterior, Caine found himself beginning to enjoy her princess routine. "Really." Smiling, he lifted her hand to his lips and kissed her fingers one at a time, rewarded by her faint tremor of arousal. "Because I'd plant one on you every time those ridiculously seductive lips got within puckering range."

" 'Plant one'?"

"Like this."

Chantal's blood swam as his lips captured hers for one more brief, fiery moment. "Oh." Pressing her finger against her tingling mouth, she imagined that she could still feel the heat, even now. Opening the compact, she frowned as she studied her swollen lips in the mirror. "Blair is a darling," she said, managing a reasonably casual tone as she struggled for composure, "but she's such an incorrigible gossip. By tomorrow, everyone in Philadelphia will believe that we're lovers."

As much as he wanted her, Caine wasn't wild about being included in the long list of Chantal's various lovers. "Does that bother you?"

"Only that it's not true." Repairing the damage as much as possible, Chantal closed the compact with a click. "I believe we're expected in the parlor for Blair's famous petits fours," she said, denying him an opportunity to respond. In truth, she was not certain that her self-esteem could handle another one of Caine's polite rebuffs.

Watching her struggle to regain her composure, Caine admitted to himself that making love with Chantal Giraudeau would be easy. But falling in love with her would be, as his grandmother O'Bannion would have so shrewdly pointed out, a completely different kettle of fish.

THE HOUSE WAS DARK. Quiet. The distant rumble of thunder echoed on the horizon. Chantal lay in bed, inhaling the faint scent of lilacs in the air as she tried to untangle her feelings for Caine O'Bannion.

She hadn't been with a man—hadn't wanted to be with a man—since the day she'd finally thrown in the towel and walked out on Greg. After the devastating years she'd spent trying to survive the sham of her marriage and the pain of the inevitable divorce, Chantal had encased her heart in a thick block of ice. It was safer that way, she'd assured herself, and she'd been right.

Then she had come to America and met a man who possessed his own personal blowtorch.

There'd be no sleeping tonight. Pushing the covers aside, Chantal rose from the bed and padded barefoot to the window. She'd just started to push the draperies aside when she heard the soft, plaintive cries of a kitten coming from somewhere behind the wall. Remembering what Blair had said about secret passages, Chantal began to run her fingers over the floral wallpaper, searching for an entrance. Nothing. Not even a ripple in the smoothly applied paper. The kitten's cries increased.

It had to be here somewhere, Chantal thought, turning on the bedside lamp. Wooden angels sounding trumpets were carved on the fireplace mantel, and as Chantal traced the lines of their gowns with her fingertips, there was a slight grinding sound and the back of the fireplace slid open. "A walk-in fireplace," she murmured. "How ingenious." Ducking her head, she entered the secret doorway.

"Here, kitty," she whispered, not wanting to wake up the other members of the house at this late hour. "Come here, kitty."

The secret passage was as dark as midnight and as cold as a witch's heart. Chantal shivered and had just about made up her mind to go back for her robe and a light when she heard the frantic mewing again. "Here, baby," she called out softly as she turned a corner that took her farther away from the light and comfort of her bedroom. "Come to Chantal. Here, kitty."

Without warning, she felt something come up behind her. Something too large, too solid to be a mere kitten. When a strong hand clamped over her mouth, forcing a scream back into her throat, she began to struggle, kicking backward with her bare feet, hitting out wildly with her hands. Her fingernails scraped a bloody path down the side of her assailant's face, and she felt his hold on her ease as he spewed off a string of harsh, guttural curses.

Just when Chantal thought she might actually have a chance to escape, something rigid came crashing down on her head. A flash of lightning exploded behind her eyes. Then everything went black.

# 9

CAINE WAS HUDDLED in the front seat of the car across the street, watching the Sherwood house.

"I hate this," he muttered.

"I don't know what you're complaining about," Drew said. "At least you were invited to dinner while your long-suffering partner was reduced to eating take-out burgers and fries."

"Anything fancier than a fast-food taco would be wasted on you," Caine countered, cringing as his partner tore open a bag of chocolate-covered raisins.

"True enough," Drew agreed with resolute good humor. "But I do thank you kindly for the petits fours."

Caine wondered if the cleaner would be able to get the chocolate frosting out of his suit-jacket pocket. "Anything for a pal. Damn, it's cold tonight." The temperature was making his shoulder ache; he rubbed it.

Drew noticed Caine's gesture. "Why don't you go back to the hotel? I don't mind pulling a little extra duty."

"I'm staying."

"Suit yourself." Drew poured them both a cup of coffee from the thermos he kept in the back seat. "Got it bad, huh?"

Caine didn't answer immediately as he took a tentative sip of the steaming, too-sweet drink. He should have known that Drew would pour half the sugar bowl into the thermos. "She's different from what I expected."

"Different good, or different bad?"

Caine considered the question. That Chantal was even more beautiful than she appeared in photos definitely lined up on the plus side of the ledger. That she was genuinely nicer and more intelligent than he'd thought were other pluses. What she was doing to his mind, however, was something he hadn't counted on. Caine decided that the unsettling feelings he'd been experiencing lately definitely belonged on the negative side. But he wasn't able to come up with any other minuses to balance out his ledger.

"Just different. You should have heard her during cocktails. The princess played that crowd like a faith healer at a tent revival. Hell, she probably collected more for her Rescue the Children Fund in ten minutes than you and I make in a year."

"Sounds as if the lady's got a future selling water purifiers if she ever decides to get out of the princess business."

"It's not a business. If you're royalty, you're royalty for life."

"And that's what's bothering you, isn't it? That when all this is over, she'll still be a princess. While you're a glorified civil servant."

"Our worlds are light-years apart."

"Did I ever tell you about my granddaddy Billy Joe Tremayne?" Drew asked, popping a handful of raisins into his mouth.

"The one who did time for shooting that federal revenuer he caught nosing around his still?"

"Nah. That was my uncle Buster Joe Tremayne. And he didn't exactly shoot him. He just winged his hat a little."

"Pumped it full of buckshot, if I remember the story correctly."

"Better the guy's hat than his head. Besides, according to the story, it was a bowler. Can you imagine what kind of blamed fool would wear a bowler in the back Tennessee hills? The way I figure it, the guy deserved what he got.

"Anyway, Billy Joe fell in love with the daughter of a family the Tremaynes had been feuding with all the way back to the Civil War. But my grandpappy could recognize quality when he saw it, and when Fayrene Drummond came home on Easter vacation from that fancy Ivy League college up north, he knew she was the girl for him. When they eloped, both families hit the roof. But nine months later, when Fayrene gave birth to my daddy, the whole thing just kinda blew over."

He held the cellophane bag out to Caine, who reached in and absently took a handful of raisins. Caine wasn't at all hungry after that enormous dinner, but stakeouts were so damn boring. "I assume there's a point to this little saga."

"Of course. The point being that every family, royalty or not, has its little differences. Differences that can eventually be overcome. Besides, you don't even know whether or not Chantal's family would object to the princess marrying a commoner."

Caine practically choked on a chocolate-covered raisin. "Who said anything about marriage?"

"A guy could do worse.... You know, life gets real humorous sometimes."

Caine tried to think of one humorous aspect of this situation and came up blank. "How's that?"

"I've been watching the two of you circle each other like a pair of my daddy's old hound dogs. Neither of you look all that dumb, yet if someone doesn't make a move pretty soon, the princess will be back home walking the floors in Montacroix, and you'll be snapping my head off in Washington. Hell, Caine, you can't deny that you're downright smitten with her."

"'Smitten'? What outdated Victorian dictionary did you get that from?" Caine muttered even as he secretly admitted the word fit perfectly.

Who wouldn't be smitten with Chantal Giraudeau? During the long, lonely nights, when he was all too aware that she was asleep on the other side of the door, he'd even fantasized about her settling down with him. But the idea of a princess marrying a guy like him was worthy of the Brothers Grimm or Hans Christian Andersen: a nice fantasy, but a fairy tale all the same.

"All right, so I'm attracted to her, okay? She's like no other woman I've ever known, and I'd love nothing more than to get out of this car right now, go up to her bedroom and ravish her until we're too exhausted and too satiated to move. Now that I've said it, will you just shut up and eat your damn chocolate-covered raisins?"

"Sure. But Caine?"

"Yeah?"

"Don't wait too long." He grinned. "She just might find out what a jerk you really are."

The night was silent; the street empty. Next door a dog began to bark and was immediately called back inside the house.

"Damn," Drew said suddenly.

Caine's own oath was just as short but harsher as he caught sight of the flickering orange light that had just appeared in Chantal's bedroom window. "Get on the horn and call the fire department," he said, throwing open the car door. "And the police. I'll get everyone out."

As he took off across the deserted street, Noel Giraudeau's nightmare flashed through Caine's mind.

THE FLASHING LIGHTS lit up the night sky. Outside, on their front lawn, surrounded by hoses, David and Blair Sherwood gathered their children around them and watched in stunned disbelief as the fire fighters worked to save their beloved house. The curious had gathered on the sidewalk across the street, watching as the flames began to lick greedily at the roof.

Inside, Drew and Caine fought their way past the powerful streams of water being sprayed from the fire trucks as they tried to find Chantal.

"Dammit!" Caine shouted, his eyes stinging from the wall of smoke as he made his way up the still-intact stairs. "What kind of woman spends a fortune on antiques but won't put out fifteen bucks for a smoke alarm?"

Drew pulled off his soaked leather jacket and put it over his head. "How about a woman who doesn't want the fire detected?"

"No way. If Blair Sherwood had anything to do with this, she would have arranged to have her kids spend the night somewhere else." The smoke was becoming heavier. The floor was growing hot beneath their feet. "Besides, you didn't see her showing off this place today. She'd just as soon cut her own wrists as torch it."

They'd reached Chantal's room. Smoke burned Caine's lungs and he began to cough. The fire had obviously begun here; the four poster was afire and flames were ravenously devouring the curtains. But Chantal was nowhere to be seen.

"She must be in the passageway," Caine said, pointing toward the fireplace. "Blair said that's the way in."

Caine and Drew exchanged a look. Both men knew that if they were trapped behind the walls when the roof collapsed it would be the end for all of them.

"Let's go," Drew said.

On the other side of the wall, Caine could feel the heat and hear the roar of the fire as it ravaged the house. The narrow passageway was starting to fill with smoke, making their flashlights almost useless. As he crawled along, feeling in front of him, he found himself making deal after deal with God.

If he could only find Chantal, he'd never sneak another cigarette again. If she was still alive, he'd call his mother once a week, whether he had anything to say or not. If he could get her out of here safely, he'd give ten percent of his salary to Chantal's beloved Rescue the Children Fund every month for the rest of his life. He might even, he promised rashly as he heard the sound of the flames whipping across the roof, try going back to church.

He was trying to think up yet another bargaining chip when his hand suddenly came across something furry. The calico kitten, terrified by the events of the night, reacted instinctively, clawing a ragged path down the back of Caine's hand. He stopped in midcurse as he bumped into a seemingly boneless bundle of silk.

"I found her," he called out to Drew, who was following closely behind.

"Is she . . . ?"

Directing the beam of his flashlight onto her face, Caine pressed his fingers against the side of her neck. "She's alive," he said, relief rushing over him.

Drew came up beside Caine and shone his own light over her, lingering on the blood staining the shoulder of her sea-green silk nightgown. "Looks like somebody bashed her a good one," he said, brushing her hair back and exposing a deep gash behind her ear.

"I'm going to find who did this," Caine vowed. His cold, quiet tone was more deadly than the loudest shout. "And when I do, I'm going to kill him."

"Why don't we get your lady out of here. Then we can worry about catching the bad guys." He ran his hands quickly, professionally over her body. "I don't think she's got any broken bones. Let's see if we can bring her to."

Caine lifted her up, cradling her in his arms. Beyond the walls the sound of the fire grew louder. Outside, the lonely wail of sirens continued to rent the air as even more fire engines arrived to fight the blaze.

"Chantal." His fingers moved over her face, stroking, gentling, comforting. "Come on, sweetheart, you've got to help us get you out of here."

Chantal opened her eyes and saw Caine, illuminated by Drew's flashlight. Even as confused as she was, she knew that she'd never, as long as she lived, forget the look on his face. There was fear there. And concern. And something else. Something so remarkable, she knew she'd have to think about it later.

"Caine?" Struggling to sit up, she began to cough. "What are you doing here? What's happening?"

"That's what we'd all like to know, Princess," Drew said. "But right now, we need to get you out of here."

She dragged her hands through her hair, struggling to understand. "I'm bleeding," she said in disbelief as her fingers encountered something warm and sticky at the back of her head.

"You're going to be all right," Caine assured her. "Do you think you're up to crawling out of here?"

"Crawl?"

"The house is on fire. The air is fresher close to the floor."

"Fire?" Her head was whirling and she felt as if an elephant was sitting on her chest. She coughed again. Once. Twice. Violently. "Oh, my God! Blair! And the children!"

"They're safe," Caine said as a sound like a freight train roared overhead. The fire was obviously spreading quickly through the attic, and they couldn't afford to waste any more time or oxygen. "Come on," he said, putting his arm around her. "This place isn't going to last much longer."

They were crawling back the way they'd come when a set of sharp claws suddenly clenched at his back. "Stupid cat," he muttered, doing nothing to dislodge the frightened kitten clinging to his shirt.

"The kitten," Chantal said. "I remember now. He was crying. He sounded frightened so I came in here to rescue him when suddenly someone came up behind me." Dizziness nearly overcame her; she stopped momentarily to let it pass. "I don't know who it was."

"We can talk about that later," Caine said grimly. "Right now you need to save your breath."

They reached the bedroom and were nearly all the way down the hallway when they heard a giant whoosh. The three of them watched in silent awe as a vast column of flames rose up to engulf the curving staircase, greedily eating away the ornately carved banister.

"So much for taking the easy way out," Drew said.

"We're going to have to jump," Caine agreed.

Chantal stared at them. "Jump? From the second story?" Her eyes were tearing from the soot in the air; her lungs were screaming for just one pure, clean breath. There was nothing she wanted more than to get out of this inferno, but surely there was some other way.

"It's our best chance, Chantal," Drew said.

"The only one," Caine said. "Come on, Princess, where's your spirit of adventure? Just hold on to my shirt. If we get separated in all this smoke, I might never be able to find you again."

Chantal couldn't believe the way both men remained so calm. So in control. "I suppose it's time I confess my single failing," she said, struggling to keep her voice steady.

She was spectacular, Caine thought. Any other woman would be screaming her head off about now. Chantal was obviously royal all the way to her fingertips. "What failing is that?"

"I'm afraid of heights."

"You are kidding."

"I wish I were."

Caine thought about her admission for only a moment. "No problem. We'll just try one of the back bedrooms," he decided. "With any luck, the terrace roof will still be intact."

Slowly, inch by inch, they made their way back down the hallway. As they passed Chantal's bedroom once again, the glass in the Palladian window exploded out onto the lawn.

It was only a bad dream, Chantal thought. A nightmare. Soon she'd wake up and find herself safe and sound in bed. Then, in just a few minutes she'd be running with Caine through the streets of Philadelphia, garnering energy for the busy day ahead.

Unfortunately, this was no dream. The flames rapidly engulfing the house were all too real. Her eyes were tearing violently from the soot and the smoke, and her lungs felt as if she'd swallowed a chestful of burning coals.

"Here we go," Drew said, leading the trio into what Chantal remembered to be the master bedroom. The heat had peeled the ivory silk paper off the walls, a layer of soot had settled onto the top of the gilded Duncan Phyfe dressing table and flames had begun licking at the colorful postage-stamp quilt covering a Sheraton field bed. "Hey, we're in luck—this room has a balcony."

The glass in the French doors had been blown out earlier. Caine crawled onto the balcony, the others close behind. "Okay," he said as he helped Chantal to her feet, "all we have to do now is jump down onto that terrace rooftop."

It was less than eight feet. Eight feet between a chance to live and the probability of dying in this inferno that only hours before had been Blair Sherwood's pride and joy. "I can do it," she said. "But we have to take the kitten."

Caine was one step ahead of her. Peeling the terrified feline off his back, he unbuttoned his shirt and stuck the cat inside. "The little troublemaker is all taken care of. Ready?"

The fire had caught on to one of the bedposts and was licking at the acorn finial. Chantal knew it would only be a matter of moments before the entire room was engulfed in flames.

"Caine?"

"Yeah?" Beneath the studied calm in his voice, she could detect an edge of impatience.

"Will you hold my hand?"

"You've got yourself a deal." Caine's strong, capable hand closed reassuringly over hers. "We'll go on the count of three, okay?"

Chantal nodded.

"One."

She took a deep breath.

"Two."

She bit her lip as the rooftop below appeared to swim.

"Three."

Closing her eyes so tightly that stars appeared behind her lids, Chantal clung to Caine's hand with all her might and stepped off into space.

# 10

SHE WAS SO PALE. Caine stood beside the gurney, holding her hand, trying not to think how close he'd come to losing her.

"I must look a fright," Chantal complained, combing her fingers ineffectually through her wet and matted hair. Behind her ear was a row of precisely sewn stitches.

Her hair smelled of smoke. Soot ringed her red-veined eyes and was smeared across her cheeks. Her bottom lip was split where she'd put her teeth through it earlier.

"You look beautiful," he said, brushing his thumb over her knuckles. The pearl-tinted fingernails of her left hand were ragged and torn.

Her laugh turned into a violent cough. "Liar," she said when she could finally speak.

As he lifted her fingers to his lips, Caine's gaze did not leave her face. "I thought I'd lost you."

His expression, along with the unmasked emotion in his eyes, made her heart clench, then begin beating all the faster. Chantal knew that the time was fast approaching when they'd have to talk about what was happening between them. But not now. And not here, in this bustling hospital emergency room, where they could be interrupted at any minute.

"Caine?"

"Yeah?"

"There's something I probably should have told you earlier."

"What?"

"My father and brother have thought for several months that someone is trying to kill me. In the beginning, I believed they were merely overreacting to a few random accidents."

"And now?"

"And now I'm afraid they may be right."

It was better to get it out in the open, Caine thought. Better for her. Better for him. He'd been frustrated by having to keep his identity a secret. So why was he suddenly so reluctant to admit to the truth?

"I think that's a good bet. And since you brought it up, I suppose I'd better warn you that the police are waiting outside to talk to you." Only by flashing his Presidential Security ID had he managed to keep them at bay this long. The president, upon receiving Drew's phone call, had dispatched a team of FBI investigators who were also currently cooling their heels in the hospital's waiting room.

She shook her head, grimacing slightly as giant boulders rolled around inside. "I don't want to talk to the police."

"Would you rather give the guy another shot at you?"

His harsh tone grated, but Chantal could read the honest concern in his eyes and decided against responding in kind.

"I'd rather just get away from here. From all this," she said quietly, waving her hand around the room. The green curtain around them was drawn, but there was no mistaking the hurried, competent activity going on in the emergency room.

In the cubicle beside them, doctors and nurses worked valiantly in a futile attempt to revive a middle-aged man's heart. Across the room the teenage victim of a gang fight had a gaping knife wound that was being attended by an emergency room intern who didn't look old enough to shave.

The world hadn't stopped spinning just because she'd almost died, Chantal realized with a small jolt of surprise. Life went on, as it always had. "Please, Caine, take me to the hotel."

"Dammit, Chantal, this is serious."

"I know. And I promise that after some sleep, I'll be much more clearheaded and able to answer all their questions in more detail."

She had a point, Caine conceded reluctantly. He'd questioned her in the ambulance on the way to the hospital, and her story had remained exactly the same: she'd followed the kitten into the hidden passage, was grabbed from behind by an unknown assailant, fought him off as best she could, and that's where all memory ceased until she woke to find the passageway filled with smoke and Caine and Drew bending over her. But still, every moment they waited, the bastard could be farther away.

Chantal reached up and put her palm on his unsmiling face. "I promise to cooperate. Once I get some sleep."

He couldn't remember ever vacillating like this. Part of Caine wanted nothing more than to take Chantal as far away from this place as possible. He wanted to escape with her to some balmy tropical island, where they'd pass the time lounging on sun-drenched beaches, sipping Mai Tais and making love.

As appealing as that idea was, Caine's professional side argued that he shouldn't be wasting time; that he should be trying to track down whoever was responsible for that wicked gash at the back of her head. Whoever it was had already tried to kill her more than once and would undoubtedly try again.

Caine covered her hand with his. "I'll try to stall them. But you're going to have to talk to them later today."

"After some sleep," she agreed. "And a shower."

Giving in, as he'd always known he would, Caine left the curtained cubicle, shaking his head in frustration to Drew, who'd just finished making the necessary telephone call to Chantal's family.

"They're coming over on the Concorde," he said.

"All of them?" Facing the entire royal family after such a devastating failure was something Caine was not at all eager to do.

"I can't imagine keeping any of the O'Bannions away if it had been Tara who'd been hurt."

"Point taken," Caine agreed, thinking of how his family had rallied around his sister during her recent divorce. "Look, do me a favor and stay with her, will you? I've got to take care of the police and those feds."

"Sure thing. And Caine?"

"Yeah?"

"This wasn't your fault, you know."

Caine's face was grim as he turned to leave the room. "Wasn't it?"

When Drew entered the cubicle, Chantal greeted him with a faint smile. "I think Caine's mad at me."

"Not at you. He's mad at himself."

She arched an eyebrow, surprised that a facial gesture could hurt. "Why? He saved my life. You both did."

Drew shrugged. "Caine's not an easy man to get along with all the time. As much as he expects from the people around him, he's always demanded even more from himself. He thinks he should have been able to protect you from whoever did this."

"That's ridiculous. Caine is a diplomat, not a bodyguard."

Drew wasn't about to touch that one. The truth was going to come out; it was better that Caine be the one to tell her. "Hey," he said instead, "I brought you a present." Reaching into his pocket, he pulled out a familiar yellow cellophane bag.

A light brightened in her red-rimmed eyes. "Chocolate-covered peanuts," she said on a pleased little laugh. "Drew Tremayne, I think I love you."

A little in love with her himself, Drew grinned in response.

"Sounds as if you two are having a good time," Caine observed as he returned.

"Look what Drew brought me," Chantal said, holding up the bag of candy.

Taking one look at the pleasure in her eyes, Caine vowed to buy out the hospital's candy machine at the first opportunity. "Just what you need after a shock—a sugar jolt. I got you sprung from here and bought some time before you have to talk to the police."

"Thank you." Her expression turned serious. "For everything."

Unable to handle the gratitude on her face, Caine turned away.

"Come on, Princess," Drew said, stepping in with a good-natured grin. "Let's blow this joint."

As they walked out the door, Chantal took a deep breath of brisk, predawn spring air. Everything was going to be all right. She was going to be all right.

IT COULD HAVE BEEN minutes. Hours. Or days. The room was dark, bathed in shadows when she finally awoke in a luxuriously appointed hotel suite. Looking around, she saw Caine seated in a chair beside the bed.

"What time is it?" she asked groggily.

"About nine in the morning."

"But it's so dark."

"Blackout drapes."

Of course. She should have realized. Sitting up, she pushed her tumbled hair away from her face and turned on the bedside lamp. "You should have wakened me," she protested. "The exhibit—"

"Is managing well enough without you at the moment. You'll be glad to know that yesterday's crowds broke the museum's opening day record."

"Yesterday's?" She struggled to concentrate. "What day is this?"

"Friday."

"But the dinner at Blair's was on Wednesday night."

"Bull's-eye."

"Then I've been sleeping for more than twenty-four hours?"

"Twenty-eight, give or take a few minutes. Those pain pills the doctor gave you turned out to be doozies. When you were still dead to the world last evening I gave him a call, and he assured me that they affect some people that way and the best thing to do would be to let you sleep it off."

"Pain pills?" That explained why her head felt as if it were wrapped in cotton batting. "But I never take pills of any kind. Not even aspirin."

"This was a special circumstance. In case it's slipped your mind, Princess, someone tried to kill you."

Remarkably, she had forgotten. Slumping back onto the pillow, Chantal pressed her fingertips against her throbbing temples. "I thought it was a dream."

Caine left the chair to sit on the edge of her bed. He lifted her hair off her neck. "These stitches are no dream. They're damn real. Just like the fire. And the faulty brake line on your Ferrari. And the roof tiles that almost hit you on the head last month. And let's not forget the way the ski trail was mismarked to lead you out onto that glacier."

Stunned, Chantal stared at him. "How do you know about those things?" When he didn't immediately answer, all the little pieces of Caine O'Bannion that she had not been able to fit into a workable whole began slipping into place.

"You're not really a diplomat, are you, Caine?"

"I work for the government."

"But not the State Department."

"No. Not state."

"What then? FBI? CIA?"

"I work in the Treasury Department."

"Doing what?"

It was now or never. "I'm a Presidential Security agent. My superior assigned me to accompany you on this tour because of what he and the president and your father perceived to be attempts against your life. I was supposed to protect you."

Stunned though she was, Chantal could still detect the self-reproach in his gritty tone. She'd have to deal with the fact that he'd lied to her later, when she'd had time to sort things out. At the moment she only knew that she hated him feeling responsible for her own stupidity.

If she'd only listened to her father, to Burke. But if she had, then she would have brought her own security force to America and she and Caine would never have met. Timing, she mused, was indeed everything.

"If you work for the president, you must be very good at your job."

"I used to think I was."

She knew she should be furious at his deception, but for some strange reason, which she'd also think about later, she could not work up the proper amount of injured pride. "Caine," she said softly, "you saved my life. Why, if you and Drew hadn't found me—"

Caine cut her off. "It never should have come to that. Especially since I had received a warning about the fire before we even left New York."

"Noel." It was not a question.

"Noel," Caine agreed grimly. "How did you guess?"

Chantal shrugged. "She has this knack. When we were children, it drove me crazy. As we grew older, I learned to listen to her." *Except once*, Chantal added silently. *I ignored all her warnings about marrying Greg.*

"She told me about a dream she'd had. About you lying in the dark, near death. She'd seen it all. The fire, the smoke." Caine dragged his hand over his face. "Dammit, I should have listened."

How could she be angry with him when he was so unrelentingly furious with himself? "What could you have done?"

"I don't know. Forced you to stay here at the hotel, I suppose, where you'd have been safe."

"But then you'd have had to tell me who—and what—you were. And I suspect you'd already given your word not to do that."

He took her hand in his. "Believe me, it certainly wasn't my first choice. Unfortunately, your father felt that since you refused to admit that your life was in danger, you'd reject any bodyguard assigned to you."

Chantal considered his statement. "Papa may have been right. I'm afraid I can be a little headstrong from time to time."

Despite the seriousness of the conversation, a half smile quirked at the corners of his mouth. "'A little'?"

"Perhaps a bit more than a little," she admitted. "Enough so that I may have indeed refused a bodyguard on principle. But that was before I met you." Her dark eyes grew wide and clouded with need as she gazed at his face. "May I ask a personal question?"

Caine willed himself to stay calm. All his life, even as a child, people had described him as a rock—unemotional, unmovable. Despite his mother's assurances that she was quite capable of taking care of them, he'd felt an unbearable need to take on the role of the man of the house after his father's death. He'd been head altar boy at Saint Gregory's, high school senior-class president, Eagle Scout, valedictorian, and to no one's surprise, had followed in his father's footsteps by going on to be cited for his sterling leadership qualities at the U.S. Naval Academy.

Even his Presidential Security assignment was a plum position, the result of hard work and an unwavering attention to duty. He'd never been a man with doubts; he'd always known who he was and exactly where he was going. He was, quite simply, a man used to charting his own course.

Until a breathtakingly beautiful princess had stormed into his life like a hurricane. During these past days with Chantal, Caine had felt hopelessly adrift, as if he'd been cast onto a dark, uncharted sea, forced to navigate by instinct alone. He was a long, long way from the controlled individual he'd always thought himself to be, and he wasn't sure he like it. Not one damn bit.

"You're entitled to one question, I suppose. Considering all the lies I've told you."

She touched a hand to his cheek. "Were you going to tell me who you were before you made love to me?"

He wanted her so very badly. And the situation was so very tempting. Caine hesitated, duty warring with desire, honor with need. Inexplicably drawn by a power more intense than anything he'd ever known, he cursed softly as he lowered his mouth to hers.

"I could never have kept the deception up," he said against her lips. She tasted moist and sweet. "Not this way."

"I'm glad." Chantal linked the fingers of both hands around his neck. "Make love with me, Caine. Prove to me that I'm still alive."

He needed no second invitation. As he slipped the narrow straps of her nightgown off her shoulders, her skin felt like liquid satin to his touch. She'd taken a shower immediately upon arriving at the hotel, and now, as his lips skimmed over the warming flesh that he had denied himself for too many days, Caine thought he could detect the lingering aroma of the gardenia bath talc the management had generously supplied. Her luxuriously soft breasts filled to fit his hands with such perfection that it crossed his mind that they might have been created specifically for him.

"We shouldn't be doing this."

She pressed her finger against his frowning lips. "This is no time to be analytical."

One final scrap of reason tried to make itself heard in the heated turmoil of his brain. "This is crazy," he said, his words a gentle breeze against Chantal's mouth.

"I know." A golden glow infused her body as he ran his tongue around her lips. She had to touch him, to experience his body as he was experiencing hers. With hands that trembled slightly, Chantal unbuttoned his shirt. "That's what's so wonderful about it. Please let's be crazy, Caine. Let's be crazy together."

Her hands fretted over his chest; her fingers tangled in the softly matted dark hair. He was taut, tense, hard as a rock. Bending her head, she pressed her lips against him, exalting in the dark, masculine taste of his flesh. Needs tore at her—wild, wanton cravings that only he could satisfy. A lingering sense of danger, fueled by desires too long ignored, created a greed she was stunned to discover she possessed.

When her fingers trailed down his rib cage, lingering over his stomach before slipping beneath the waistband of his jeans, Caine decided that if this was madness, sanity was highly overrated. Passions that had been building for days threatened to consume him; the memory of how he'd felt when he'd thought he'd lost her made him ache.

"Chantal." It was only her name, but never had she heard it sound so sweet. "Chantal . . . Chantal." He said it over and over again, a lush litany of wonder.

A ruthless, ripe hunger consumed them both. Chantal heard the sound of silk tearing and welcomed it. Caine's own clothing disintegrated as if blown away by a fierce desert whirlwind. The crisp sheets beneath them became a heated tangle; the cool air grew hot and steamy.

If this was insanity, Chantal welcomed it with open arms. Her hands, like her lips, refused to remain still as they roved over his body, never lingering in any one place as they teased and tormented. In turn, Caine was relentless, nipping and licking and sucking, as if he wanted to leave no part of her body untouched, unclaimed.

He'd intended to treat her like a lady. Like a princess. But she'd bewitched him from the beginning, and now he finally succumbed to her with a primitive kind of desperation he'd never known before.

Chantal wrapped her legs around him and drew him into her, thinking that having him inside of her was more than she'd ever want. Or need.

"Chantal." His breath fanned the hammering pulse in her throat. "Open your eyes, sweetheart. I want to watch you go over the edge."

Unable to deny him anything, Chantal did as he asked. Her eyes were full of restless pleasure as he began to move, slowly at first, then deeper and faster, taking her places she'd never known. She arched against him, agile and demanding, moaning softly as she reached her peak. But Caine was relentless, and incredibly the need built again, higher, hotter, until her body went wild, matching the power and speed of his.

Caine watched her eyes darken to molten amber as she gave herself to him totally. And when she peaked again, he allowed himself to follow.

"I REALIZE this will sound terribly trivial to a man," she murmured, wrapped in Caine's arms, "but I'm relieved that I let you talk me into taking only the clothes and jewels I planned to wear in Philadelphia to Blair's house. I would have hated to have had to replace everything on such short notice."

"Speaking of jewels, they're going to be sifting through the ashes, but I wouldn't hold out a lot of hope for those amethysts."

"They're insured. Fortunately, I never take this one off."

Caine took hold of her hand, toying with the slender silver ring. "I've been wondering about this."

"Burke gave it to me. On my parent's wedding day. The day we legally became brother and sister."

"Your brother sounds like a nice man."

"The nicest." Subject closed, Chantal smiled at him. "Have I told you that I love your body?"

She was remarkable. Other than the faint shadows under her eyes and the row of stitching at the back of her head, there were no signs that she'd been on the brink of death. "I don't believe the subject's come up."

"I do." She pressed her lips against his chest. "Every morning when we're out running, it's all I can do not to drag you into the nearest alley and have my wicked way with you."

He tangled her hair in his hand, pulling her mouth to his. As he drank from the honeyed sweetness of her lips, Caine wondered if he'd ever get enough of her. "It's a good thing you managed to resist the temptation. The police are an unromantic bunch. They tend to frown on public displays of lust."

"I suppose your superior might also disapprove of such behavior," she said, slipping lower to continue her tantalizing assault down his body. How she loved his dark, musky scent!

"Probably fire me on the spot." Her tongue plunged wetly into his navel, and Caine drew in a sharp breath.

"Then you'd have no choice but to come to Montacroix and be a royal guard."

Alarms sounded in his head. "Chantal...."

She'd pushed too far. Burke had always chided her on her impatience. Damn, she thought, struggling to ease the tenseness from Caine's body with hands and lips, when would she learn to curb her natural impulsiveness?

"I was only joking," she soothed, not quite truthfully. Actually, the idea, which she honestly hadn't thought of until this moment, sounded wonderful.

Caine observed her carefully, looking for some hint of a prevarication. What they'd shared was special. Unique. But unfortunately, it hadn't changed a thing.

Dear Lord, she really was in danger, Chantal realized suddenly. She was in danger of falling in love with Caine. Perhaps she already had. If that was the case, he could hurt her now. He could tear her heart to ribbons, and this time she might not recover.

"Honestly, Caine, I don't expect a lifetime commitment from you. I'm entirely willing to accept a short-term relationship. A no-strings affair that will last only as long as I'm in your country."

Even as she heard the words leave her lips, Chantal knew they were a lie. She wanted more from him, a great deal more. But afraid of frightening Caine away, she tried to make herself believe that she would be satisfied with whatever he was willing, or able, to give.

Just when he'd come to believe that Chantal was not the fall-in-bed-at-the-drop-of-a-hat princess of the supermarket tabloids, she did a 180-degree turnaround and invited him to enter into a one-night—or in this case, eight-night—stand. It was such a rapid reversal that Caine felt as if he should ask the real princess to please stand up.

"No strings," he repeated dubiously, running his hand down her side from her shoulder to her thigh. Her skin was warm and soft, and she trembled under his light touch.

Her heart was drumming. Her blood warmed. Would he always be able to affect her this way? With a single touch? A mere look? "No strings," she said.

Caine's hand settled on her hip, his fingers molding to the slender bone as he remained silent for a long, thoughtful moment. Experience had taught him that nothing in life came totally unencumbered. "Is that really what you want?"

"Isn't it enough?"

Caine tried to accept her answer for what it was: a declaration that the only future he and Chantal had together was a brief, fiery affair that would last just as long as her time in the States. Wasn't that exactly what he'd wanted?

So why did he suddenly find the idea strangely distasteful?

"Do you honestly believe that it's enough?"

Because she wasn't entirely sure of the nature of her own needs, Chantal could not understand his. "Really, Caine," she protested on a forced laugh, "must you take everything so seriously?"

"I take you seriously." With fingers that were heartbreakingly gentle, he brushed her hair back from her forehead, wondering what childhood adventure had resulted in that thin scar over her eye and wishing he'd been there to prevent it. "I wish I didn't. But I can't help it."

Even as she warned herself against setting herself up to be hurt again, Chantal felt a tiny seed of hope taking root in her heart. A hope that would make her vulnerable. Dependent. All the things she'd sworn she'd never be again.

"Is that so bad?"

"I don't know," Caine said on a long breath. "I just don't know." He shaped her shoulders with his palms. Just looking at her made him want. Touching her made him ache.

Chantal didn't resist as he drew her into his arms. As their mouths met, they went together to a shimmering, glowing place where there was no need for answers.

# 11

CHANTAL WAS IN THE SHOWER when the phone rang. "O'Bannion," Caine answered it.

"Hey, Caine," Drew said without preamble, "I just thought you might want to know that I'm with the Giraudeau family now. Their plane has landed a little ahead of schedule, and we should be arriving at the hotel in thirty minutes or so."

Thirty minutes. Hardly time to take care of one last item of business, let alone try to explain to Chantal why he was going to leave her. Well, Caine considered, it had been nice while it lasted. But it was time to return to reality.

"Thanks. Could you do me one more favor?"

"Sure."

"Stay with them until my replacement arrives."

There was a long pause on the other end of the line. "Be glad to," Drew said finally.

"Thanks."

Hanging up the receiver, Caine dragged his hand wearily over his face. Chantal was still in the shower; he could hear her singing over the sound of the water running. Part of him wanted to join her under the streaming warm water, to make love to her one last time. Another more responsible part of him cautioned against it.

Picking up the phone again, he placed a long-distance call to Washington.

"Believe me, Caine," James Sebring said after listening to Caine's request, "the fact that Chantal found out about your little deception and didn't throw a tantrum makes me even more convinced that you're the perfect man for the job. The princess has never taken well to authority figures. Her agreeing to remain under your protection proves that you've a talent for handling her."

That was definitely one way of putting it, Caine decided grimly. "Sir, you don't understand," he tried again. "Things aren't as simple as they were."

"Now that you are no longer having to pretend to be someone you're not, I would think things would be a great deal less complicated," the director countered.

"No disrespect intended, sir, but there is nothing uncomplicated about Chantal." Perhaps it was the way he'd said her name—a softening of his tone, a lingering over the musical sound. Whatever it was, the director's next words gave Caine the impression that he'd revealed far more than he'd intended.

"Do you know," Sebring said slowly, thoughtfully, "I seem to recall Chantal's father, Prince Eduard, saying much the same thing about her mother thirty years ago."

"I don't believe you understand, sir," Caine protested.

"On the contrary, I believe I understand all too well." There was another long pause. "I appreciate your dilemma, Caine. I also know that you're an honorable man and will do the right thing. Including keeping the princess safe."

He decided to try one last time. "I believe I could be more effective tracking down her assailant." As he'd sat beside her all those long, lonely hours, watching her sleep, Caine had decided to find the man who'd done this to Chantal, to ask for a personal leave of absence in order to get the job done.

"That's not your duty, Caine," the director said firmly.

"I want this man, sir."

"So do we all."

"If you'd only assign someone else to the princess—"

"While you're an exemplary agent, I'm ordering you to leave the detective work to the FBI. Is that clear?"

Caine had worked at the agency long enough to realize when arguing would be futile. "As a bell, sir."

Chantal was still humming when she exited the bathroom, a fluffy peach bath towel wrapped around her. As she heard Caine requesting to be relieved of his duty, a dark, spreading pain started in the pit of her stomach. He couldn't want to leave her. Not after all they'd shared. Some men might take whatever a woman was offering, then vanish. But not Caine. Please, not Caine, she begged, pressing her hand against her left breast, where the hurt threatened to take root.

He'd no sooner hung up when Caine heard a slight sound behind him. Turning, he viewed a frighteningly ashen Chantal standing in the doorway. "Are you all right?" he asked, hurrying to her side. "Is it your head?"

With a calm that belied the turmoil battering away inside her, Chantal met his concerned gaze with a level one of her own. "My head is fine."

"You're too pale."

"Honestly, Caine, I'm fine."

The heat that had been practically emanating from her earlier was gone, and she'd cloaked herself in a sheet of ice. Strange, Caine considered, he would not have thought Chantal had it in her to be cold.

"You're angry with me."

Afraid of her tumultuous emotions, Chantal wrapped her arms around herself in an unconscious gesture of self-protection. "I am not."

He put his fingers under her stubborn chin and tilted her head up. "Yes, you are. And I'll be damned if I know why."

"You're imagining things, Caine. Just let it be."

Tempted to shake her, Caine grasped hold of her arms. "No. Not until I get a straight answer."

"You were arranging for a replacement," she said, jerking free. "Tell me, Caine, did you also expect this replacement to share my bed? Is that one of the perks of being an executive bodyguard?"

He'd hurt her. Badly, it seemed. Caine wondered if he could do anything right where this woman was concerned.

"Chantal, listen to me." He put his arms around her, holding her when she tried to resist. "What we've shared the past few days is very important to me. Not just the lovemaking, although that was definitely a highlight, but all of it. Even the arguments. And to tell you the truth, although I'm not at all sure how I feel about what's happening between us, I could never take it—or you—lightly."

His hands moving up and down her back cajoled as his lips against her temple soothed and excited at the same time. "You were going to leave me," she murmured into the hard line of his shoulder.

"I was going to explain later, after I made the arrangements."

"For your replacement. So you could go back to Washington."

"I wasn't going back to Washington."

She tilted her head back, studying him gravely. "You weren't?"

"No. I wanted to track the man down who did this to you. To make him pay."

A host of emotions coursed through her, thrilling and terrifying at the same time. She reached up and traced the ridged line of his jaw. "I hadn't realized a professional could feel the need for revenge."

"That's pretty much what Director Sebring said when I asked for a change of assignment." What Caine hadn't told the director was that while he was crawling through all that smoke, he'd realized that the need to protect Chantal had stopped being professional long ago.

"Does that mean he refused?"

"Turned me down flat."

"Then you're staying with me? Until the end of the tour in Los Angeles?"

Conflict raged in him. He wanted to leave now, while his heart and his life were intact. At the same time he wanted to lock the door, take Chantal to bed and spend the rest of his life making wild, passionate love to her. *Go. Stay.* The words reverberated inside his brain until he thought he'd go mad.

"Until Los Angeles," he agreed, lowering his head. When his lips touched hers, ambivalence disintegrated. "Now, if you don't get some clothes on, Princess, I'm going to forget that your parents will be here in less than half an hour."

Her family. How could she have forgotten that Caine had told her they were flying to America? "I suppose I should warn you."

"Warn me about what?"

"My father is a very perceptive man. If he suspects that there is more than business between us, I'm afraid you may be in for a parental grilling."

"Don't worry about it. I was a Seal before I joined Presidential Security."

"A seal? Like the sea animal?"

"The navy's special forces. They trained us to survive torture techniques, so I can probably handle whatever your father might think up."

Chantal sighed. "It is obvious that you do not know my father."

THE FIRST THING Prince Eduard Giraudeau did upon entering Chantal's suite was to embrace his daughter in a huge bear hug. Then he turned toward Caine, his hands on his hips, a dark glower on his face. "You're O'Bannion."

Caine would have had to have been deaf not to hear the accusation in Chantal's father's tone. "I am," he replied.

"Both your president and James Sebring assured me that you would protect my daughter."

"Papa, Caine saved my life," Chantal protested. "He and Mr. Tremayne risked their own lives to get me out of Blair's house before the flames completely gutted it."

Eduard harrumphed. "If he'd been doing his job properly, you never would have gotten yourself in such a fix in the first place," he insisted, not taking his fierce eyes from Caine's.

"You're not telling me anything I haven't told myself a million times since it's happened, Your Highness," Caine said.

Easing the awkward moment, Burke stepped forward. "I believe introductions are in order. I'm Chantal's brother, Burke. This is our mother, and I believe you've spoken with Noel."

As he stood face-to-face with Burke Giraudeau, Caine felt as if he were being thoroughly summed up. The younger prince had a lean, intelligent face and dark eyes that looked as if they never missed a thing. After shaking hands with Chantal's brother, Caine turned toward Jessica. "I've always admired your work, Mrs. Giraudeau. I wish we were meeting under any other circumstances."

Jessica smiled. "Why, thank you, Mr. O'Bannion, although I wouldn't think you'd be old enough to remember any of my movies."

"His father was in love with you for years," Chantal offered.

"Really." Her pleasure was obvious. "I'd love to meet him. Perhaps, when all this is over, if your mother wouldn't mind."

If anyone else had made such an offer, he would have thought it to be nothing but an attempt at polite conversation during a difficult time. But Jessica seemed sincere. A nice woman, he decided. And even more beautiful than she'd appeared to be on the late show. "My father died several years ago. But I appreciate the offer. Your films gave him a great deal of enjoyment."

Caine turned to Noel. "Princess," he greeted her, nodding. He observed the two sisters standing together; they were a study in contrasts. Chantal's dark, sultry looks brought to mind rich Gypsy laughter and blazing camp fires. Noel's silvery-blond hair and bluish-violet eyes reminded him of a cool alpine stream rushing through flower-strewn meadows.

Noel's smile, in its own way, proved every bit as devastating as her sister's. "Please," she said, extending her hand. Her unlacquered nails had been buffed to a glossy sheen. "I thought we'd already settled on Noel."

As their fingers touched, Caine realized from the look in Noel's eyes that she intuitively knew that he and Chantal had been intimate. Caine's own gaze instantly became shuttered.

Noel's glance was sympathetic as she looked over at her sister.

"You needn't have come all this way," Chantal told her family as she took a seat. "As you can see, I'm quite well."

Jessica Giraudeau poured a cup of tea from the pot that had been delivered by room service immediately after their arrival in Chantal's suite. A superb arranger, Jessica had used the cellular telephone in the limousine to order a light meal on their way to the hotel from the airport.

"You're as lovely as ever, darling," she agreed, holding the cup out to her daughter. "But when one has a shock, one needs family close by."

As she took the proffered cup, Chantal thought of all the other times her mother had come to her rescue with a steaming cup of tea. To Jessica, tea was a magic elixir, soothing everything from a headache to a broken heart. "You are all wonderful."

A slight frown furrowed the smooth line of Jessica's brow as she watched Chantal stir a second spoonful of sugar into her tea, but she held her tongue. "It was all I could do to keep your father from hijacking the airplane in his hurry to cross the Atlantic."

"They had no business holding the flight up like that," Eduard complained. "I explained the importance of our mission, but the imbeciles refused to listen." Volatile, outspoken, the prince radiated a lingering frustration that had Chantal sympathizing with the Air France flight crew.

"They listened, Papa," Noel corrected mildly.

"Then why did they refuse to take off?"

"Perhaps the fact that the airport was engulfed in a cloud of fog had something to do with it," Burke said dryly. He was perched on the arm of Chantal's chair. "How are you, really, little one?" he asked, brushing her hair away to examine her stitches.

"I'm fine. Really," she insisted as he gave her one of the long, probing looks that had always been her undoing. "Better than fine."

"When we find the monster who did this," Eduard said, "I will insist that the legislature bring back the guillotine." He narrowed his eyes in warning to anyone who might want to argue the point. Understanding that he was still afraid and loath to show it, everyone remained silent.

"And now that we have dispensed with the social amenities, Mr. O'Bannion," the prince said, turning back to Caine, "would you care to tell us exactly how you plan to protect my daughter during the remainder of her time in your country?"

"Actually, I've been trying to convince your daughter that she should cancel the rest of the tour. But she's proven rather immovable on the subject."

"Chantal has always known her own mind," Eduard said with the air of a man who might constantly fret over his daughter's intransigence but refused to hear a word of criticism from anyone else.

"Tenacity is one thing," Caine said. "Pigheadedness quite another."

"'Pigheaded'?" Chantal said on a furious gasp.

"Just calling them like I see them, Princess."

It took a major effort, but Chantal resisted stamping her foot. "I am not pigheaded. And don't call me Princess."

The impending fireworks were obvious, as was the electricity arching between them. Seeing the blazing fury in her daughter's eyes, Jessica stood up and put her hand on her husband's arm. "Darling, I am suddenly so tired I can barely stand. I'm afraid that jet lag has caught up with me. Would you mind escorting me to our room? Perhaps later we can all get together and discuss Chantal's plans."

"But you never have jet lag." He pressed the back of his hand against her forehead, checking for fever. "Perhaps you've taken ill."

"I'm merely tired," she assured him. "I'll be fine after a rest. Perhaps you'd care to join me."

Eduard looked back and forth between Caine and his wife, as if struggling to make a decision.

"You can speak with Mr. O'Bannion later, darling," Jessica suggested adroitly. "When you're not behaving like a hysterical father."

"Why shouldn't I be?" he grumbled. "That's what I am. But you have a point, as always, my dear. I will allow you to cajole me into behaving in a more civilized fashion."

"Thank you, Papa," Chantal said.

He drew her into his arms, pressing his lips against her hair.

"I love you, *chérie*," he said gruffly, his deep voice wavering. His dark eyes were suspiciously wet.

Chantal's own eyes were none too dry as she put her arms around her father, allowing his solid bulk to comfort her. "And I love you. All of you," she said on what was nearly a whisper as her loving gaze took in her mother and brother and sister.

Caine watched, strangely moved by the scene. He'd been attracted to Chantal from the beginning, but even as he'd begun to admit his feelings to himself, he'd tried to concentrate on her fire, her smoldering sex appeal. Now, as he watched her with her family, saw her in the role of daughter, sister, he had an inkling of another Chantal. A strong, loving woman who, oddly enough, reminded him a bit of his mother.

"I really am sorry I hurt you," Caine said once they were alone again.

"You needn't apologize, Caine. I overreacted."

Caine reached out and twisted a few glossy, dark strands of her hair around his fingers. "I should have realized how you'd take my leaving right after we'd made love."

"It wasn't your fault. Actually, it was more of a knee-jerk reaction dating back to my ill-fated, highly publicized marriage." Her smile, as she looked up at him, wobbled ever so slightly. "Greg had a habit of disappearing."

To his surprise, Caine felt a jolt of something that uncomfortably resembled jealousy at the mention of her former husband.

"I suppose that's not so surprising for a Grand Prix driver." He wondered if Chantal had objected to her husband's traveling in order to earn his own living. Had she honestly expected him to remain in the palace like some royal lapdog? "The racing circuit covers most of the world."

"I wouldn't have minded the racing. It was his extracurricular activities I found hurtful."

"The guy played around?" What kind of idiot would stray when he had this sexy, passionate woman waiting for him at home?

Appearing suddenly uncomfortable, Chantal crossed the room, where she stood looking out the window. Her suite had a breathtaking view of the Logan Circle gardens, but she was not seeing the brilliant flowers. Instead, her vision was directed at a scene several years and many miles away.

"The first time was on our honeymoon. Greg was scheduled to race in the Monaco Grand Prix the following week, so we'd rented a villa in Eze. A small Riviera village between Monaco and Beaulieu," she explained at his questioning look. "It's a lovely, quiet, intimate little place, perched high on a hill, with cobbled streets and medieval houses topped with dusty red-tiled roofs, all removed from the hustle and bustle of the social hubs like Saint-Tropez and Monte Carlo."

"Sounds like a great spot for a honeymoon," he said, coming up to stand beside her.

"That's what I thought. Until I returned from the market, where I'd bought the most luscious fresh strawberries I'd planned to dip in melted chocolate. Greg had teased me about not being able to cook, so I'd bought a cookbook and had decided to begin with the desserts."

"Knowing you, that makes perfect sense," he agreed, kissing her because it had been much too long.

"Mmm," she murmured happily as her lips clung lingeringly to his. "I do so love the way you kiss, Caine."

"You're not so bad, yourself, Princess. So, while you were out at the market, practicing to be a dutiful little housewife, your husband was home boinking the maid."

"She was not a maid but a singer from the cabaret we'd visited the night before," Chantal corrected. "But yes, he was indeed—" the unfamiliar but easily understandable colloquialism slipped her mind "—whatever it was you said."

"You should have kicked the bastard out on the spot."

"I'd just taken my marriage vows three days earlier."

He took her icy hand in his, his thumb brushing lightly across her knuckles. "So had he," Caine reminded her, choking back a very strong urge to curse the man Chantal had married. "Don't they have women's liberation in Montacroix?"

"Of course, but when you grow up with parents who love each other the way mine do, you develop some very strong ideas about what a marriage should be. And one of those ideas is that you shouldn't run away the first time things get a little rough."

"Another rule of thumb is that you don't screw around on your spouse."

"I know." She gave a long sigh that rippled through her. "But in a way, you see, it was my fault."

"I find that difficult to believe."

"Not only couldn't I cook, but I wasn't very good at the physical part of marriage, either," she admitted with a low, strained voice he had to struggle to hear. There, she'd said it. Hearing the words out loud didn't make them less painful, she discovered.

Caine stared disbelievingly. "You are kidding."

"Not at all." She could feel the color rising in her cheeks. "I was a virgin when I married Greg."

"Did he know that?"

"Of course. Oh, I'd dated other men before him, although not nearly as many as those horrible tabloid newspapers alleged. I'd even been engaged briefly once, and during my teens I'd had a wild crush on Burke's cousin, Stephan Devouassoux. But I had been taught that lovemaking was something special, to be shared with that one person you wanted to spend your life with, and although such a belief always seemed natural to me, my virginity did tend to scare more than one man away."

"Their loss."

Chantal smiled. "Thank you."

He shrugged. "It's the truth. But Greg was different?"

"He said he admired the fact that I had such high standards, that I had, as he put it, saved myself for marriage. You've no idea how happy those words made me. I thought, finally, after all those years, I'd found someone who shared my feelings."

A slight frown crossed her face. "Burke tried to talk me out of the wedding. He said that Greg was the kind of man who would view an untouched bride as the ultimate challenge. That once I was no longer a virgin, his passions would cool and he'd be back to his hedonistic life-style."

"Sounds as if your brother hit the nail on the head."

"Greg did have other women. But only because I couldn't please him."

Caine felt a blaze of anger. "Yeah," he said, kissing her furrowed brow, then her temple, "you're a real bust in the sack, Princess. That's why I can hardly move."

"It was good, wasn't it?" she murmured wonderingly.

"*We* were good," he corrected, trailing a lazy finger down her face. "You and I. Together."

She sighed as his lips skimmed over the trail his finger had blazed. "Together." It was happening again, she thought wonderingly as she felt her bones melting.

Need. Hunger. Want. Her body seemed to respond instinctively to his, warming at the touch of his hands, softening at the feel of his lips.

Forever, Caine mused as fresh desire rippled through him. He could make love to this woman forever. He was prepared to do precisely that when the phone began to ring.

"Ignore it," she murmured, her hands combing through his dark hair.

"I can't. It might be important." With a low oath, he reached over and picked up the receiver. "O'Bannion.... Yes, sir. She's right here." He handed the phone to Chantal. "It's your father."

"Hello, Papa," she said, exchanging a look of regret with Caine. "Of course I can be ready in half an hour.... Yes, I'll tell him.... Papa, don't you dare do any such thing.... Papa, I'm warning you.... Damn," she muttered. "He hung up."

"Problem?"

"I'm afraid so." Her expression was gravely apologetic. "Papa insists that you join us for dinner."

"I'd like that," he surprised her by saying.

"Really?"

"Really. Perhaps before this evening is over, between the two of us we can convince you to cancel this damn tour."

"You know I can't do that. The children are depending on me."

"The children don't expect you to set yourself up as a target," Caine shot back. "What I should do is simply refuse to let you leave this room until we catch the guy who's trying to kill you."

Chantal tossed her head. "You'd have to tie me down first. And you'd never do that."

"Want to bet? I've got a set of handcuffs in my room that are probably just your size."

"You're a bully, Caine O'Bannion."

"That's one way of looking at it. Personally, I prefer to think of it as doing my job, but I suppose you're entitled to your own opinion."

"I know you. You aren't serious about those handcuffs."

"We could put it to the test, if you'd like."

She studied him for a full ten seconds. Finally, a slight smile began to tease the corners of her lips. "Did anyone ever tell you that you are incredibly sexy when you start throwing your weight around?"

"All the time," he lied deftly. "How about you? Did anyone ever tell *you* that you're enough to drive the average man to drink?"

Her gaze met his in a softly challenging way. "But you're not the average man, are you Caine?"

He took a moment to answer, struggling against the sensual invitation he read in her dark eyes. "I like to think I'm not," he agreed, his casual tone taking a Herculean effort. "Now, if you think you can manage to stay out of trouble for five minutes, I want to change into a suit before dinner."

As he reached the doorway of the bedroom, Caine turned. "Whatever you do, don't open this door to anyone," he instructed, trying to conceal how desperate he was to keep her safe.

As he quickly changed out of his jeans into a charcoal-gray business suit, Caine wished once again that he could take a more active part in the investigation surrounding the fire that had come so close to taking Chantal's life.

From the moment she'd been deliberately lured into the secret passage and struck, there'd no longer been any question that someone was willing to go to extraordinary lengths in order to arrange her death. But who? And why?

Caine could only hope that they found the answers before her would-be killer struck again.

THE DARK-HAIRED MAN swore at the television screen as he watched Chantal give a brief statement to the throng of avid reporters gathered in the porte cochere of her hotel. That the authorities were calling the fire an unfortunate accident was not surprising; an act of attempted murder would create an international incident, something the governments of both Montacroix and the United States would want to avoid at all cost. The investigation would be done surreptitiously.

As he watched the princess and studied the grim-faced man in the gray suit standing beside her, the man cursed himself for not realizing from the beginning that her escort was a great deal more than a mere lower-echelon diplomatic drone.

Pointing the remote control toward the television, the man vowed that after Chantal, Caine O'Bannion would be the next to die.

# 12

"ALONE AT LAST," Chantal said with a sigh of relief as she and Caine returned to her suite later that evening. "I truly love my family, but it was becoming quite exhausting having them hover over me like a clutch of anxious mother ducks."

"Hens."

"Whatever. I thought I'd die when Papa announced that he was joining us for the remainder of the tour. Thank goodness you were able to change his mind and convince him to return to Montacroix."

"I only pointed out that his presence would make my job more difficult."

"It was the way you did it." Chantal looked at him with undisguised admiration. "For a moment there, I was almost able to believe you were the diplomat you originally professed to be. Papa is not the easiest of men."

"It's obvious that he and the rest of your family love you. It's also obvious that they're worried sick about you continuing this tour."

She kicked off her high heels and sank down onto the couch. "Please don't start in on that again."

"In on what? Would you like a drink?"

"Brandy would be nice," she agreed. "And you know very well what you're doing. You're trying to make me feel guilty about causing them concern."

As he poured brandy into a pair of balloon glasses on the bar, Caine glanced over at her curiously. "Would it work?"

"No."

"I didn't think so," he said, crossing the room and handing her one of the glasses. "But it was worth a shot." He sat down beside her, sipping the brandy, enjoying one of the few peaceful moments they'd managed to share during the past fourteen days. "I like your family. They're not what I would have figured them to be."

"And how had you thought of them? As a group of pompous, autocratic, self-important, wealthy snobs?"

Caine shrugged. The description hit too close to home for comfort. "I haven't had much of an opportunity to mingle with royalty."

"We're people, just like everyone else."

"Now that's where you're wrong, sweetheart," he murmured, running a hand down her hair, remembering how the long, dark strands had felt draped across his chest. "Because you are not like anyone else."

His eyes, as they settled on her face, were as intense and dark gray as a storm-tossed sea. Chantal took a deep breath and exhaled quickly. "I'm afraid," she whispered through lips that had gone uncomfortably dry.

"You should be. Someone's been trying to kill you."

She shook her head. "Not of him. Of us."

Caine managed a grim smile. "You're not alone there, Princess."

"Caine." It was only his name, but it spoke volumes. "What's going to happen? To us?"

What indeed? Caine wondered. In the beginning, he'd tried to tell himself that his attraction to Chantal was purely physical. And although he'd wanted to keep their relationship strictly professional, he had assumed that if the opportunity ever arose to act on what was obviously a mutual attraction, his desire would be satisfied, his hunger satiated. It had been a logical assumption, based on past experiences. And Caine was nothing if not a logical man.

But something had gone wrong. Because instead of easing his need for her, their lovemaking had only served to make him more greedy. Somehow, when he wasn't looking, he'd crossed the line between want and need.

"Now you sound like your father."

His feigned humor didn't fool her for a moment. He was as disconcerted by all this as she was, Chantal realized. And why not? That he hadn't wanted this assignment in the first place was obvious; that he hadn't wanted to become emotionally involved with her, even more so.

Patience had never been Chantal's strong suit, yet every instinct she possessed told her that nothing would be settled by forcing the issue. They both needed time to think, to reassess the changes in their relationship. She only wished they could do so without the additional stress of the tour, and of that man, whoever he was, wherever he was, trying so hard to kill her.

"Actually, you were quite fortunate," she said. "Every time Papa opened his mouth to interrogate you, the others came riding to the rescue like the heroes in all your American Westerns."

"Noel makes a rather interesting Clint Eastwood."

"Wasn't she amazing?" Chantal asked, warming to the subject of her sister. "I had no idea she could be so forceful. Imagine her interrupting Papa like that! Again and again. She had him so frustrated, I worried that he'd explode before we finished dessert."

"Still waters..." he murmured. "I got the distinct impression that you two are more alike than you seem at first glance."

Chantal looked up at him with renewed interest. "Really? Most people don't see any resemblance at all."

"You don't look anything alike," he conceded, "although you're both stunningly beautiful. But I was talking about what's inside—those iron-strong wills you both share."

His perception pleased her. She'd made the mistake of falling in love with a shallow man once before; she was glad that Caine was a man who took nothing at face value. "In her own calm way, Noel can wear away a stone."

"Yet she couldn't change your mind."

She heard the aggravation in his tone and knew that his grievance was shared by her family. "I'm not going to let him win," she said in a firm, quiet voice. "I'm not going to begin living in fear just because some crazy person out there doesn't like me."

Her fingers curved around his upper arm, and her expression was intense as she tried to make him understand. "Don't you see? Like it or not, I'm a public person, and if I allow this man to send me scurrying back to the safety of Montacroix, I'll never be free of him. I'll have to spend the rest of my life hiding out in the palace, surrounded by armed guards."

Fear for her safety, plus something that was beginning to feel more and more like love with each passing day, made his words rash. "Not the rest of your life, dammit. Just until we catch the guy."

"And when you do, then what?"

"Then you can resume your tour."

"But what if I receive yet another threat? What would you have me do then?"

Even as he knew where this conversation was leading, that in her own single-minded way, she made sense, he still didn't like the idea of her setting herself up as a target for some madman.

"Don't you understand? I care about you."

The turbulent emotions she saw swirling in his eyes nearly took her breath away. "Don't worry about me. I'm under the protection of the president's personal body-guard."

"A fat lot of good that did you the other night," he said grumpily. He'd known all along that he wasn't going to change her mind, but he never would have forgiven himself for not trying.

"Please, let's not think about that tonight," she coaxed prettily, her eyes amber pools of need as she took his empty glass and placed it on the table in front of them along with her own. "Or tomorrow." She reached up, freeing him from his red silk tie. "Let's pretend there's only now. Only this one perfect night together."

There were plans he'd intended to discuss with her, cautionary changes in her itinerary that would help ensure her safety, but as she manipulated the buttons of his white dress shirt, releasing one after another until she was able to press her hands against his bare chest, Caine lost the ability to concentrate.

"Tonight you're mine," he said in a low, deep voice rough with emotion.

"Yours." She gasped in surprise as he pulled her down onto the plush carpeting, but then she wrapped her arms around his neck and clung, eager to go anywhere he wanted to take her. "All yours."

CAINE WOKE FIRST, which allowed him the pleasure of watching Chantal sleep. Her lips were curved in a softly satisfied smile, which made him wonder if she was dreaming of the love-filled night they'd shared. A shaft of morning sunlight streamed into the room through a slit in the heavy draperies, illuminating the exquisite planes and hollows of her face.

Although his body was sated, his mind was not. How was it, Caine asked himself, that each time he made love to Chantal only made him want her more? What had begun as normal male desire was rapidly escalating to something that more and more resembled obsession.

Murmuring low, inarticulate sounds of pleasure, she turned toward him, her blissful sigh unmistakable as she pressed her body against his. Imbued with an uncharacteristic feeling of tenderness, Caine touched his lips to her sleek, dark head, content to lie quietly with her in his arms.

"What time is it?" Chantal murmured groggily into his shoulder. She tightened her arms around him, fitting her slender frame even more closely to his.

"Time to get up." He lifted her hair and pressed a kiss against her neck.

"Mmmph." She burrowed deeper, reminding him of a fox settling into its den. "I'd rather stay here. All day. With you."

"We have a plane to catch, remember?" In no real hurry to move himself, Caine idly played with her hair, sifting the dark strands through his fingers like grains of sand.

"We can always make a later one."

"We're due in Milwaukee at noon."

Unwilling to return to the real world quite yet, Chantal rolled over and straddled him, moving in such a way that the friction between their bodies seemed to create sparks in the early-morning light.

"How much time do we have, exactly?"

Caine's fingers dug into her hips as he lifted her up and settled her over him. "Enough," he said as their bodies merged and their minds entangled.

THE PHONE CALL came as they shared a hurried breakfast in the suite. They were due at the airport in a little more than an hour.

"That was Drew," Caine said as he returned to the room service table.

"Oh?" Chantal looked up from buttering her sweet roll. "Please tell me that our flight's been canceled. That we have nothing to do but spend the rest of the day in bed, where I can have my wicked way with you."

Caine shook his head with good-natured disbelief as he sipped his coffee. "Lord, lady, you are insatiable. Don't you ever get enough?"

"Of you?" She gathered the scattered crumbs from the roll into her palms. "Never. I'm afraid you've ruined me for any other man, Caine," she said cheerfully as she brushed the crumbs onto her gold-rimmed plate. "Years from now, when I'm a little old silver-haired lady, sitting in my rocking chair in some retirement home for aged royalty, I'll still be lusting after your magnificent body."

Caine felt a stab of guilt at Chantal's reference to the future. He had always been forthright with the women he'd become involved with; his romantic relationships were based solely on shared interests and mutual physical pleasure. Then Chantal had come into his life, and he'd started contemplating a future with her even when he knew one could never exist.

"Well, I'm sorry to disappoint you, but he was calling about business. He has a line on your assailant."

"Really? Who is it? Does he know?"

He put his napkin down and leaned back in the chair. "Unfortunately not. What the FBI guys did uncover was how he managed to get into the house in the first place."

"How?"

"As one of the waiters."

"But I thought you told me you and Drew had checked out the caterers before we arrived in Philadelphia."

"We had. Unfortunately, several employees called in sick with the flu that day, so there were a lot of last minute changes. Enough that no one realized one of the waiters had been paid a substantial amount of money to disappear."

"How does Drew know that?"

"The FBI caught the guy boarding a plane to Jamaica. With a hundred thousand dollars in cash."

"Someone paid all that money just to take his place?"

"Seems so." Caine's expression was grim. "The bureau is sending a police artist to the airport so we can help them work up a composite of the counterfeit waiter."

Chantal vaguely recalled a tall blond man with a neatly trimmed beard. A man who had seemed oddly familiar at the time, but intent on raising funds for her charity, she hadn't fully focused on him.

"Caine, one of the waiters was on the plane from France with me."

Every atom in his body went on red alert. Finally, something to go on. "Are you sure?"

"Positive. He kept staring at me through the entire flight."

"Why the hell didn't you tell me that in the first place?"

"Because at the time it didn't mean anything. I am quite accustomed to men's appreciative glances."

"Too bad you can't tell the difference between honest masculine lust and murderous intent."

It took an effort, but Chantal assured herself that Caine's gritty tone was solely due to concern for her safety. "You may find this difficult to believe, but accepting the idea that someone actually wanted to kill me was extremely difficult," she said quietly.

Caine knew he was being hard on her, but he couldn't help himself. If she'd only call off this damn tour...and what? Return to Montacroix? Was that what he really wanted?

"Well, hopefully once we get an accurate sketch, we'll be able to get a line on the guy."

The idea of all that money kept reverberating around in her head. "Caine?" Her cheeks were paler than they should have been, her dark eyes shadowed with an unmistakable dread.

"Yeah?" He took her hand in his across the table.

"Whoever he is, he's very serious, isn't he?"

Dead serious, Caine thought grimly. "Yeah," he said instead, "I think he is."

"But why didn't he just poison my dinner? Wouldn't that have been easier?"

"It also would have been too fast. There would have been no way to poison you and get out without drawing suspicion to himself."

"How did he know about the secret passages?"

"That's an easy one. Remember Blair telling us that her home had been designated a historical landmark and that the blueprints are on file at the historical society?"

"Vaguely."

"Although only members and scholars are admitted to the archives, one of the volunteers recalls a telephone repairman recently working in the room where the prints were filed."

Chantal fell silent for a long time, absently tracing circles on the crisp white linen tablecloth. "Surely this is not the work of a single man?"

"We don't think so."

"I don't understand. Why would anyone conspire to kill me?"

"I don't know." His fingers tightened on Chantal's. "But I swear, Chantal, that we're going to find these guys. And when we do, they're going to pay."

She didn't want to think about it. It had to be a mistake, some bizarre practical joke gone berserk. But as she watched determination harden Caine's eyes to cold, gray steel, Caine knew that this was incredibly, terrifyingly real.

ALTHOUGH CHANTAL had been to America several times, her visits had been confined to the coasts: New York, Los Angeles, with an occasional trip to Palm Springs and Palm Beach. Now, as she and Caine traveled across the vast country, she was discovering a myriad of surprises.

Milwaukee, which had always brought to mind beer and babushkas, proved to be a surprisingly cosmopolitan city, boasting an encyclopedic art museum containing collections ranging from ancient Egyptian to modern American. She was proud to have her own work displayed in such august company and pleased when the city proved more than a little generous when it came to contributing to her charity.

It was while she was in Milwaukee that Chantal received a jolt back to the past in the form of a telephone call from someone who had, for a brief time, been the most important man in her life.

Stephan Devouassoux was technically Burke's cousin, not hers, but he'd always seemed like a member of the family. Except for those turbulent teenage years when she'd had a raging crush on the tall, handsome Cambridge student.

"Stephan," she said delightedly, "how on earth did you track me down?" After the fire, her hotels had been changed and the new locations kept a closely guarded secret.

"I finally managed to convince Burke to give me your itinerary. Honestly, Chantal, his behavior reminded me of a mother bear guarding her cub."

"Burke's been worried about me."

"And rightfully so, which is why his overprotective attitude failed to insult me. How are you, *chérie*? Ever since I read about that terrible accident in Philadelphia, I've been worried sick." His voice over the long-distance wires possessed the same deep, velvety warmth that had succeeded in melting her youthful heart.

"I'm fine."

"Are you certain?"

"Positive." When Caine, seated in a chair across the room, scowled a warning, Chantal remembered that the official story was that the fire had been an accident. What no one but a select group of insiders knew was that the various empty gasoline cans discovered in the rubble had served as mute proof to the contrary.

"But you were hospitalized."

"Only for observation."

There was a pause. "Well, I shall be relieved to see for myself that you did, indeed, escape that horrible fire unharmed."

"'See for yourself'?" A smile claimed her face. "Don't tell me that you're in Milwaukee."

"Correct country, wrong state. I'm in Los Angeles and I have purchased a ticket for your exhibit."

"That's wonderful! But I thought you were living in Paris."

"I was until two years ago. I was approached by a group of individuals while attending the Cannes Film Festival. They were seeking funding to form an independent production company in Los Angeles, and since Paris had become boring, predictable, I decided to give California a try."

"And is California less predictable and boring?"

He laughed heartily. "What do you think?"

"I think, Stephan dear, that California would suit you perfectly. You always were the most flamboyant member of the family."

"Heaven knows I've done my best. But we all know that ever since your fifth birthday, I've come in a distant second to the most beautiful princess in the world."

She laughed at that, as she was supposed to. When Caine narrowed his eyes at the soft, musical sound, Chantal felt a surge of feminine power at the idea that he could become jealous.

Caine pointed down at his watch. "If we don't get going," he whispered, "we're going to miss the opening pitch."

Although he hated the idea of allowing her to mingle with the public, when Chantal decreed that she couldn't begin to understand his country until she had experienced America's national pastime, Caine had relented, agreeing to take her to a night baseball game.

Chantal nodded her acquiescence. "Stephan, I'm afraid I must run. But it was wonderful to hear from you, and I can't wait to see you in Los Angeles."

"On the contrary, *ma chère*," Stephan countered with that old-world gallantry she had once found so irresistible, "it is I who will be waiting with bated breath to see you. *Au revoir*, Chantal."

"*Au revoir*, Stephan," she said softly. She was still smiling as she hung up the phone.

"Stephan. That's the cousin, right?" Caine asked. "The one you thought you were in love with."

"It was a crush, nothing more."

"Did I hear you say you were meeting with him in L.A.?"

"He's coming to the gallery," she confirmed.

"Why?"

"Obviously to see me. We were once very close."

Caine arched a brow. "Exactly how close?"

"Are you jealous?"

"Of course not," Caine countered, not quite truthfully. As a matter of fact, he hadn't liked the way her expression had softened while she was talking to this alleged cousin. "Now, if you're ready, Drew has the car waiting downstairs."

As they took the elevator to the lobby, Caine decided to check out this Devouassoux character. It was only a hunch, but Caine had learned long ago to trust his instincts. Besides, if he was going to suddenly have a rival for Chantal's affections, he wanted to know what he was up against.

IN YET ANOTHER COMPROMISE, Chantal had reluctantly agreed to watch the baseball game from a private, glassed-in box at County Stadium, which precluded her mingling with the fans as she would have liked. There she discovered to her delight that beer and bratwurst were de rigueur in this town that still reflected a rich German heritage.

Chantal had always considered herself an intelligent woman. Even so, the game taking place on the diamond of bright green grass remained a mystery. Deciding that the smartest thing to do was simply groan and cheer along with the crowd, she found herself enjoying the evening immensely. Despite the fact that besides Caine and Drew, she'd been accompanied by a detail of blue-suited, unsmiling FBI agents.

"I'm sorry for the fans that their team didn't win tonight," she said later as Drew drove them back to the hotel. "And although I understand their disappointment, I find it difficult to believe the umpire was actually blind."

Plucking a peanut from the red-and-white striped bag she'd bought at the game, she cracked the shell and popped the meats into her mouth. As she crunched her expression was one Caine would have expected to see from a woman sampling imported caviar.

"He wasn't, was he?" she asked hesitantly. "I mean, surely that isn't possible."

"Of course he wasn't. And don't worry about the fans. If there wasn't at least one questionable call per game, they wouldn't have anything to talk about until the next one. It keeps interest up."

"Oh." Chantal pondered that for a time, deciding that it made sense. "Caine?" she said at length.

"Yeah?"

"May I ask you a question?"

"Sure."

"Have you ever been married?"

"No."

"Why not?"

From the way he dragged his hand through his hair, Chantal decided that it was not his favorite subject. "When I was in the navy, my work consisted of doing the kind of covert stuff that can end up being dangerous. I didn't think it fair to ask a woman to share that risk."

"And later?"

He shrugged. "Same story."

"But surely there are other navy men and Presidential Security agents who are married?"

"Sure, but they didn't grow up without a father. Having been that route, I swore never to inflict it on my own kids."

From his gritty tone, Chantal knew enough not to argue. "Have you ever thought about having a family?"

"Hasn't everyone?"

"What would it be like?"

He glanced down at her, half irritated, half amused. "What is this? I feel like I'm getting the third degree."

"You know about my marriage," she protested softly, understanding his tone, if not the exact meaning of his words. "I was just curious how you felt."

Caine linked his fingers behind his head and leaned back, considering her question. It had been so many years since he'd allowed himself to think about marriage that an answer didn't come immediately to mind.

"Marriage," he mused aloud. "Let's see. First of all, I'd live in the country."

"Not the city?"

"The city's no place to bring up kids."

"Then you do want children?"

He looked over at her sharply. "I thought this was a hypothetical question."

"It is," she said quickly. "So, if you were to get married, which you do not intend to do, you would want a home in the country with children."

"And a dog for the kids. None of those fancy little fuzzy toy things that spend all their time in dog beauty parlors. A real dog—an Irish setter or a golden retriever. Maybe a German shepherd."

"It sounds as if you'd need a very large house."

At the mention of houses, Chantal experienced a stab of guilt at the thought of Blair's lovely home. Fortunately, only the upstairs had suffered extensive damage, and with the help of the original blueprints, Blair and David intended to restore the house to its original glory. Chantal had talked to her friend only this morning, and although Blair had waxed enthusiastic about having a new project to embark on, she could not disguise the sadness in her voice. Immediately upon hanging up, Chantal had telephoned Burke in Montacroix, asking him to arrange for an unlimited line of credit with a prominent Philadelphia antique dealer.

"It should be roomy," Caine agreed. "Although nothing like what you're accustomed to. And it'd be white, with a wide front porch for watching your neighbors, rose bushes in the front yard and a big tree in the back for a swing."

"And what of your wife? What would she do with her days while you are out being a hero?"

He considered her question for a long moment. "She could work outside the home," he decided. "So long as it didn't interfere with her family duties."

"'Family duties'? Cooking, cleaning?"

"Hell, no, we'd all pitch in with that household stuff. No, I was talking about the important part of a marriage. Loving me. And letting me love her."

Chantal drew in a breath. "It sounds wonderful."

Caine laughed, obviously embarrassed that he'd permitted a rare glimpse of his innermost thoughts. "It's not bad," he agreed. "For a hypothetical."

"For a hypothetical," she agreed quietly.

"One more thing."

"Yes?"

"It'd be a decided plus if she could darn my socks."

"I think it's a good thing you aren't really looking for a wife, Caine. That sort of thing went out with covered wagons."

"What are you talking about? I'll have you know, my mother used to darn my socks."

"Then why don't you simply send your holey socks to your mother?"

He grinned. "She gave it up the summer I turned twelve. I seem to recall her saying something about having always hated the job and me being old enough to take care of my own clothes."

Chantal laughed. "Your mother sounds like a very wise woman."

"The best," Caine agreed.

A comfortable silence settled over them.

"I had a wonderful time tonight, even if I couldn't understand all the logistics of the play," Chantal said after a time. "Thank you for taking me."

It had begun to rain in the bottom of the eighth inning, the moisture cooling the evening temperatures. The woodsy scent of oakmoss and sandalwood bloomed enticingly in the warmth of the car heater. Had it not been for Drew sitting in the front seat, Caine would have taken her into his arms and satisfied the hunger that had been escalating more and more with each succeeding inning.

Instead, he tugged lightly on the ends of her dark hair. "It was my pleasure," he said simply, meaning every word.

DENVER ALSO PROVED a city of contrasts. Having always thought of Colorado as a state consisting solely of rugged, snowcapped mountains, Chantal was surprised to discover that the mile-high city appeared to be situated on land as flat as a tabletop. To the east, rolling plains that seemed to go on forever gave the city an aura of isolation. To the west, the Rocky Mountains gave the city its mystery and brought to mind the gold and silver mining camps that had contributed to Denver's wealth.

She found the city's pioneer legacy strongly evident at the Museum of Western Art, which among action classics by Charles Russell and Frederic Remington, boasted pieces from the famed Taos school. For those who might tire of so many horses, the Denver Art Museum, where Chantal's exhibit was displayed, boasted one of the best contemporary collections in the United States.

"This is an amazing country," she said over a buffalo steak dinner at a restaurant founded by one of Buffalo Bill's scouts. She'd just finished making certain that the paintings were properly recrated and on their way to the state of Washington, where they would be on exhibit at the Seattle Art Museum Pavilion.

"I've always thought so," Caine agreed.

"It's so large. And the diversity is dizzying." She glanced around the dining room. An astonishing herd of animal trophies—bison, elk, caribou, moose—gazed unblinkingly down from the wall.

"I imagine Montacroix is more homogeneous."

"Vastly so. But, of course, it's a very small principality. And most of its citizens share the same roots." She grew pensive, pushing her home fried potatoes around on her plate. "Some people might find such similarity comforting."

"While you, on the other hand, find it stifling," Caine guessed.

"A bit," Chantal admitted on a soft little sigh. "Although I don't want you to think that I don't love my country. It's just that lately, as I've begun to expand my painting, I've also found myself wishing for more . . ." She paused, seeking the proper English word for her feeling. "Space."

"Elbowroom."

"Excuse me?"

"Have you ever heard of Davy Crockett?"

"Of course. He is an old American hero, is he not? The man who wore the cap made from raccoon skins?"

"That's him. Anyway, old Davy wasn't much for civilization. Professing the need for elbowroom, he kept moving farther and farther into the Tennessee wilds."

"Elbowroom," Chantal murmured, pondering the term for a long, drawn-out moment. "I like it," she decided. "And you're right, that's exactly how I feel." She gave him a warm, appreciative glance. "Perhaps it is my American half who feels the need for this elbowroom."

"Perhaps. But it's the Montacroix princess who'll return home after the tour."

His words of warning had the effect of tossing cold water on what had been a vastly enjoyable day. The people of Denver had expressed appreciation of the works she'd brought to America with her, and she'd raised a great deal of money for the children, which was, of course, the important thing, she reminded herself.

"Are you angry with me?" she asked.

"Of course not."

"You seem cross."

"I was just worrying about making it through the next few days without any additional surprises," he said, not quite truthfully. "If I was short with you, I apologize. It doesn't have anything to do with us." His abrupt tone signaled that he considered the matter closed.

Well, at least he was admitting that there was an *us*, Chantal mused on the way back to yet another hotel. Although she'd been booked into the largest suites in the finest hotels in each city, they'd begun to blur together in her mind. Only those hours she spent making love with Caine in the king-size beds stood out in riveting detail.

She'd given the matter a great deal of thought, trying to discern why it was that her days, no matter how long or wearying, were brighter with Caine in them, why her heart sang at the mere sight of him and her bones melted at his touch. Why was it that the sound of his laughter, which came more easily with each passing day, possessed the power to thrill her all the way to her toes? And how was it possible to feel more intimacy sharing a box of over-salted popcorn with Caine at a baseball game than she'd ever felt sharing a bed with Greg?

The answer, when it had finally come, in a plane thirty thousand feet over Manhattan, Kansas, had been as simple as it had been frightening. She was in love with him. And although she'd vowed after her marriage that she would never again risk her heart, she knew that there was no point in fighting it. She loved Caine. And she wanted to spend the rest of her life with him.

"I'm becoming quite spoiled," she murmured once they were alone in her room. She was no longer inhibited by the fact that Drew occupied the room next to hers, while in the room across the hall two FBI men kept a watchful vigil.

"Oh?" He didn't resist as she pulled his tie from around his neck and tossed it onto a nearby chair. "In what way?"

Chantal pushed his jacket off his shoulders. "I'm discovering that I can't imagine a life without my own private bodyguard." She was gradually learning not to be disturbed by the shoulder holster and gun he wore constantly outside of the hotel rooms.

Caine shrugged out of the leather holster. He wanted to warn her that she'd better start facing reality, that their time together was rapidly coming to a close. But when she gently nudged him onto the turned down bed and began divesting him of shoes and socks, he decided that once in a while it didn't hurt to simply relax and go with the flow.

"And here we were all sure that you'd balk at the idea of a bodyguard."

For a woman who'd worried about not knowing how to please a man, Chantal had all the instincts of a first-class courtesan, Caine mused. He couldn't remember the last time a woman had massaged his feet. In fact, now that he thought of it, no one ever had.

"You should have given me more credit." Tugging his shirt free of his slacks, she proceeded to undress him with tantalizing slowness. "I know a good thing when I see it." Between each freed button, she pressed her lips against his newly bared skin. "Or taste it."

His shoulders were wide, strong, able to carry heavy burdens. His arms were subtly muscled, offering comfort and protection, as well as passion. His hands were broad, his fingers long and lean and capable of discovering flash points on her body she'd never known existed.

Once she'd freed him of his shirt, her clever fingers moved to the waistband of his navy slacks.

"What do you think you're doing?"

Her smile as she slid the slacks down his legs was positively beguiling. "Why, I'm seducing you, Caine," she murmured, tossing the slacks carelessly onto the chair. They slid to the floor; neither Chantal nor Caine noticed. She ran a ruby-tinted fingernail up the inside of his thigh. "Is it working?"

"You tell me." His arousal, straining against his white cotton briefs, was impossible to ignore. Chantal brushed tantalizing fingers over him, pleased by his resultant tremor.

Stepping away from the bed, she pulled her dress over her head, letting it fall into an emerald silk puddle at her feet. Her lacy ivory bra was next, followed in turn by a pair of lace-banded, thigh-high silk stockings and her shoes. She hitched her thumbs into the top of her outrageously skimpy underpants and slid them slowly down over her hips, never taking her seductive gaze from Caine's face.

The rising passion in her eyes tore at his self-control; needs pounded inside him. "You realize that in the old days you could have been burned at the stake for being a witch," he said, his voice unnaturally husky.

"Don't be silly." Her smile was lascivious as she knelt beside him on the mattress and brushed her lips against his. "They never burned witches in Denver."

Her hands as they traced the contours of his body caused his blood to swim. When she pulled away the briefs in order to lightly brush that part of him aching for her touch, Caine had to grit his teeth. "Sure of that, are you?"

"My tour book mentioned nothing of such practices."

Bending over him, she rained a trail of wet kisses down his chest to his taut, hard stomach, and when her lips grazed his hipbone, Chantal heard Caine's desperate voice call out to her. But she was too fascinated with her quest, too intent on exploring this heady sense of feminine power she'd discovered, to reply.

Her hands fluttered over him like delicate birds, never still as they explored, relishing the hard, lean lines that were so different from her own soft, swelling curves. Her lips pressed lingeringly, warming his flesh, heating his blood, even as she caused her own fires to burn higher.

"Lord, Chantal," Caine muttered as her tongue stroked the straining sinews of his thighs. He reached for her, but she evaded his grasp.

"Too soon," she said as her avid mouth tasted his warm, moist flesh.

Passion flowed over them as she continued to torment and tease. It was an exercise in both devastating pain and dazzling pleasure. Caine wanted Chantal to keep touching him forever; he never wanted her lips to stop skimming over his aching, throbbing body. He wanted to take her now, quickly, before he completely lost his mind. The heat was unbearable; it was exhilarating. Every ragged breath he took was an agony of effort.

Seizing her shoulders, Caine pressed her back against the mattress and surged into her with an intense blaze of passion. Chantal shuddered when he first filled her, then, wrapping her legs around him, she lifted her hips, meeting him thrust for thrust.

Reality dimmed, sanity shattered. When she cried out his name, Caine's body shuddered with release, and he knew that he would remember this moment always.

# 13

SEATTLE, WASHINGTON'S Emerald City, gleamed like a jewel beside the quiet waters of Puget Sound. In the distance, the glacier-covered Mount Rainier rose through the morning fog, looking for all the world like a giant upside-down ice-cream cone.

"It's all the water that gives the city its mysterious blue glow," Chantal said, leafing through her guide book in the hotel suite. From the luxurious corner room in the high-rise tower, she possessed a dazzling view of the waterfront.

"Fascinating."

"The city is cradled by two mountain ranges—the Olympic to the west, the Cascade to the east."

"I'll try to keep that in mind," he said absently.

Caine was not in the most gregarious of moods. Not only had thoughts of Chantal kept him from sleeping, but when he had finally drifted off early this morning, he'd had a strange, surrealistic dream about the two of them starring in a colorized remake of that swashbuckling classic, *Captain Blood.*

And if that wasn't enough, Noel had called again, warning him not to let her sister go near the beach. Ever since their arrival in Seattle yesterday morning, he had worried that Puget Sound might contain the beach in question. Unfortunately, Noel's image had been frustratingly unspecific.

"The San Juan Archipelago consists of more than 170 islands scattered across Puget Sound, offering sailing, kayaking, fishing, beachcombing and bicycle riding. That last would be fun, don't you think? It's too bad we aren't going to be staying in the city longer."

"Yeah, too bad."

"But perhaps we could go to dinner on the pier after tonight's mayoral reception. Unless you'd rather hire a boat and go out into the sound and attempt to catch the killer shark that has been terrorizing the city."

"Whatever you want." It took a moment for Chantal's words to sink in. "'Killer shark'? What are you talking about?"

Crossing the room, she sat down on his lap. "You haven't been listening to a word I've said."

"Of course I have."

Chantal had a choice. She could challenge that outrageous statement or accept his word at face value, even knowing that he was not being entirely truthful. They'd been getting along so well lately, she decided against entering into an argument.

"It is a lovely city," she murmured. Turning her gaze away from his carefully guarded face, she looked out the window. The sound was filled with white sails fluttering in the wind. How she'd love to be down there with them— with Caine—sharing a chilled bottle of champagne, the sunlit afternoon and the fresh sea breeze.

"Agreed." He brushed his fingertips down the front of her crimson blouse. The silk was soft, but Caine knew her skin was softer. "I'm sorry if I wasn't paying strict attention."

Chantal had already discovered that Caine was not a man to apologize easily. Or often. "You have a lot on your mind."

Wasn't that the truth? In the beginning, the three weeks had seemed an eternity Caine was forced to endure. Now, as their time together came to a close, the days seemed to have sprouted wings. If only they had more time. . . .

For what? he asked himself. What difference would a few days make? Would she suddenly stop being a princess? Would he win the lottery? Inherit a million dollars from some reclusive, eccentric relative he'd never known he had? Besides, although he didn't want to admit it, the chasm between him and Chantal had little to do with money. Although it would take some getting used to, he could probably live with a rich wife, even if she was a princess. What he couldn't—wouldn't—do, even for her, was change who he was. What he was.

"You're worried," she said quietly.

"What, me worry?"

He was smiling, but Chantal could see the seeds of concern in his eyes. "It's going to be all right. *I'm* going to be all right," she said. He'd retreated behind those emotional barricades she'd reluctantly come to accept even as she felt her own need to breach them. "After all," she added, allowing her hand to brush through his hair, "I have a hero watching out for me."

"Drew never should have told you about that," Caine muttered grumpily.

"You wouldn't tell me how you'd injured your shoulder," Chantal reminded him. She had wondered about the angry red scar from the beginning, but when she'd asked him about it, she'd received such an abrupt dismissal that he hadn't dared bring it up again. "He's your friend. I think he wanted me to know how dedicated you are to your job. So I could understand that it's only your rigid professionalism that sometimes has you acting like Captain Bligh."

He lifted a dark brow. "'Captain Bligh'?"

She pressed her hand against his cheek. "You have been known to be a bit bossy."

"'Bossy'? Me?"

"Well, you can't deny that you're always issuing orders."

"Orders you always refuse to obey," he reminded her.

"Not always. Actually, I was thinking just this morning how good we were getting at compromising."

"'Compromising'." That was not Caine's favorite word. To him it meant giving in, something he'd been doing with increasing frequency lately. He'd tried to tell himself that he had no choice, that if he laid down the law too hard, Chantal would just go off in another more dangerous direction. But to be perfectly honest, Caine had to admit that he was simply finding it more and more difficult to deny this woman anything.

"You remember how to compromise, don't you, Caine? I give a little." She leaned forward and kissed him. "You give a little." Her lips plucked enticingly at his grimly set ones. "And after a while we're both compromised."

Her low gurgle of sensual laughter caused desire to ripple beneath his skin. "You're incorrigible."

"And you love it," she countered, linking her fingers behind his neck. Their lips met and clung. "Caine?"

"Mmm?"

"You were a sailor, weren't you? Before you joined Presidential Security."

"I was in the navy. But I wasn't the kind of sailor you see in those old World War II movies."

"Oh." She seemed momentarily disappointed. "But do you like to sail?"

"Sure. Why?"

"Although Montacroix is a landlocked country, we do have a lovely lake—Lake Losange, or Diamond Lake," she translated for him. "When I was just a little girl, Burke taught me to sail on it. Perhaps, when all this is over, you can visit Montacroix and go sailing with me."

Caine struggled not to give in to the pull of Chantal's velvet eyes. "I don't know if that would be such a good idea."

He'd withdrawn again. Although she lacked her sister's psychic gifts, Chantal was intuitive enough to realize that the stone wall Caine kept erecting between them had been a lifetime in the making. She was foolish to believe she could have permanently breached those parapets in three short weeks. But tenacity, and her newly found love, made her want to keep trying.

"When the tour ends in Los Angeles two days from now, your assignment will be successfully completed."

"Let's hope 'successful' is the operative word."

"You would not permit it to be anything less," she said, striving to keep a light tone. "Then, when it is over, you will return to Washington and I will go home to Montacroix."

"That's the plan."

Chantal took a deep breath, garnering courage to ask the next question. "We won't ever see each other again, will we, Caine?"

Caine knew he'd had no business getting mixed up with Chantal. Despite what she'd said about only wanting a short-term affair, he'd come to know her well enough to realize that despite her flamboyant public image, she was a warm, loving, happily-ever-after kind of woman. And as sophisticated as she appeared decked out in gleaming satins and sparkling diamonds, he could also envision her in a pair of brief white shorts and a cotton shirt, her dark hair blowing in the breeze, laughing with easy delight as she taught her children how to sail before the wind on Lake Losange. She deserved a man who could give her a stable, loving home, a family. Unfortunately, he was not that man.

"I don't see how it could be any other way, Chantal," he said at length, not wanting to give her any false hope.

"I see." It took a concerted effort to keep the tremors from her voice.

"We both knew this was a transitory affair," Caine pointed out.

As she read the finality in his eyes, Chantal slid off his lap with a sigh. "Of course, you're right," she said, staring unseeingly out the window at the scene that only moments before had provided such pleasure. "I hadn't realized that inviting you to Montacroix for a platonic visit would breach our agreement."

"There wouldn't be anything platonic about it," Caine argued. "We both know what would happen . . . what always happens."

"Would that be so bad?"

Caine gripped the arms of the chair to keep himself from going to her. "It would only complicate things even more."

"And you're a man who doesn't like complications," she murmured, more to herself than to him. "Is that all I've been to you, Caine?" she asked, turning around to face him. "A complication? A screwdriver thrown into the perfectly tuned machinery of your life?"

"Monkey wrench," he muttered.

"What?"

"It's a monkey wrench, not a screwdriver, and surely you realize that you mean a helluva lot more to me than that."

She'd known from the beginning that Caine was a man
capable of restraining his emotions, of holding them back
from himself and others. He was a difficult man to know,
and an even more difficult man to love, but she'd fallen in
love with him anyway. And heaven help her, she couldn't
stop just because he was breaking her heart.

"Obviously not enough."

Unable to resist the silent appeal in her eyes, Caine
pushed himself out of the chair and went over to her.
"Look, Chantal, you're a terrific woman. The way you
make me feel is probably illegal in at least a dozen states,
and I'd love nothing more than to spend the rest of my life
making mad, passionate love to you."

The idea sounded wonderful to Chantal. "But . . . ?"

"But the truth of the matter is that I'm enough of a real-
ist to know that such a fantasy would never work. We're
two different people, Chantal."

"Actually, I think we have a great deal in common," she
felt obliged to point out. "We're both single-minded, cautious in our relationships with other people, extremely
loyal to our friends and family. . ."

"That's not what I'm talking about."

She arched a sable brow. "Oh?"

"Our life-styles are too different."

"If you mean because I live in a palace and you live in
an apartment, that could be altered."

He narrowed his eyes. "I couldn't move to Montacroix.
I have my own life here in the States, my work. I would
never live off a woman."

"I don't believe I asked you to," she snapped. Taking a
deep breath that was meant to calm but didn't, she added,
"I was suggesting the other alternative."

Caine realized she was striking back because she was hurting, and he didn't blame her. Still, he couldn't even begin to take her suggestion seriously.

"That you move into my apartment? With me?"

His look was frankly incredulous and, Chantal was forced to admit, none too inviting.

"Forget I mentioned it," she said, turning away from his piercing gray eyes. "It was a foolishly romantic suggestion, obviously brought on by jet lag, too much stress and not enough sleep." Marching into the adjoining bedroom, she slammed the door behind her with enough force to cause the Matisse print on the wall to tilt.

Dragging his hands through his hair, Caine told himself it was going to be a very long two days.

THE MAN WAS DRINKING champagne out of a crystal flute as he stood at the window and stared out over the sparkling, sun-gilded water. At first he'd been furious when his carefully conceived plan had failed in Philadelphia. Now, however, he realized that he'd been wrong to assign Karl to the job.

Fate had decreed that he be the one to kill the princess. And that's precisely what he was going to do.

Tomorrow.

Here, in Los Angeles.

CHANTAL HAD ALWAYS ENJOYED everything about Los Angeles. The brilliant, almost intoxicating sunshine, the golden beaches, the lushness of Beverly Hills, the quirky individualism of Venice, the nostalgic, neon glitz of West Hollywood, the glass high rises looming above Century City like monolithic sculptures, the palm trees—all of it made her feel as though fairy tales could come true.

This time, however, the sun-drenched city did little to lift her spirits. Although her exhibit drew thousands to the J. P. Getty Museum in Malibu, and she managed to raise unprecedented funds for her favorite charity, Chantal couldn't shake the depression that had settled over her.

It was all her fault, she told herself as she smiled her dazzling smile and exchanged cheek kisses with a famous actress who had enthralled three generations of movie-goers. Caine had been totally honest with her; he'd warned her up front that he was not promising a future.

But she'd been foolish enough to think that she could change his feelings about commitment. Chantal berated herself even as she laughed at the punch line of a talk-show host's joke. She'd mistakenly believed that love conquered all. There was the real joke.

And on top of everything else, having learned his lesson concerning Noel's premonitions, Caine had canceled Chantal's excursion to Catalina Island. Needless to say, she had not been pleased.

"Better watch out," a deep voice murmured in her ear, "or your face will freeze into that scowl."

Spinning around, Chantal's face lit up in the first honest smile she'd given anyone in the past forty-eight hours. "Stephan," she said delightedly, embracing him, "I'm so glad to see you!"

"Not as happy as I am to see you," he said, his teeth a brilliant flash of white as he grinned down at her.

"It was so good of you to come."

"Personal reasons aside, you don't think I'd miss an opportunity to donate to those orphans of yours?"

"They're not all orphans," Chantal corrected. "But thank you. Every little bit helps."

Reaching into the breast pocket of his Saville Row suit, he pulled out a piece of folded paper. "Then let me add my little bit."

"Gracious," she said, her eyes widening as she stared in shock at the amount of the check. "Stephan, have you gone mad?"

He chuckled, running his knuckles down her cheek. A few feet away, as Caine watched the intimate gesture with narrowed eyes, jealousy twisted his gut.

"Of course I have not gone mad," Stephan Devouassoux answered with mock indignation. "Fortunately, *ma chère*, since moving to California, business has more than surpassed my expectations. Enough so that I can share the wealth with the loveliest woman I know."

She tucked the check into her beaded bag. "You are an angel."

"And you look like an angel." He plucked a pair of champagne glasses from the tray of a passing waiter and handed her one. "Have you ever thought of returning to films?"

"As much as I enjoyed my acting days, I was much younger then," she said. "I've become a more solitary person than the acting profession permits. Painting suits me, Stephan. I enjoy it. And I'm good at it."

He laughed, raising his glass to her in a toast. "I've always appreciated a lady who knows her worth. You know, Chantal, seeing you here today, I realize that I should have kept closer tabs on my cousin's baby sister. You've grown into quite a delectable woman, *chérie*."

As Caine watched the man's eyes practically stripping away Chantal's slender black dress, he decided that the time had come to put in an appearance.

"Is everything all right?" he asked, coming up beside her.

She tilted her chin in a way that reminded him of that haughty princess who'd handed him her luggage tags a mere three weeks ago. Had it only been three short weeks? It seemed like a lifetime.

"Everything is fine," she said frostily.

When she didn't look inclined to introduce him to the guy in the obviously tailor-made suite, Caine decided to take the bull by the horns. "The name's O'Bannion."

"Devouassoux," Stephan returned, looking curiously from Caine's closed face to Chantal's equally unreadable one and back again. "Stephan Devouassoux."

The name rang an instantaneous bell. "You're the cousin."

"*Oui*, I am Prince Burke Giraudeau's cousin," Stephan answered, his eyes revealing his surprise. "His mother, Princess Clea, was my aunt." He glanced over at Chantal. "Your friend seems to know a great deal about our family."

"He's not a friend. He's my hired bodyguard," she said, her tone heavily laced with sarcasm.

"A bodyguard?" Stephan's aristocratic features revealed concern as he took her hand in his. "Don't tell me that you are in danger, *ma petite*?"

Although Stephan's touch no longer stirred her blood as it had when she was young, Chantal couldn't deny that Caine's blistering glare was more than a little satisfying. In no hurry to retrieve her hand when it was causing Caine such obvious distress, she smiled up at her brother's cousin. "Mr. O'Bannion seems to think so," she said. "Although his judgment has been known to be impaired."

Although she'd coated herself in enough ice to cover Jupiter, the anger in Chantal's tone was unmistakable. "It's suddenly so crowded in here," she said, slanting Stephan her warmest, most feminine smile. "Why don't we take a nice stroll in the gardens?"

Turning her back on Caine, she led Stephan toward the French doors at the end of the room. Incensed by her cool dismissal, Caine held his tongue and followed.

"Your Mr. O'Bannion is quite intimidating," Stephan said once they were outside. The bright green hedges lining the walks were neatly trimmed; sunlight sparkled invitingly on the water in the long, rectangular pool.

"He is not *my* Mr. O'Bannion," she said with more intensity than she'd intended. "And he can be quite pleasant if you catch him in the right mood."

"When is that? Once an aeon?" Stephan glanced nervously over his shoulder to where Caine stood between a pair of tall white pillars, back rigid, arms folded across his chest. In deference to the bright sun, he was wearing a pair of dark glasses, but it was obvious that his gaze was fixed unerringly on Chantal. "At least you are well protected," he decided. "I can't imagine anyone trying to harm you with that man hulking in the background. I take it he's always with you."

"Day and night." Except for the past two nights, when he'd slept on the couch outside her bedroom door, she silently added. At least he was supposed to be sleeping; listening to him pace the floor had provided Chantal with a small amount of selfish pleasure. It was gratifying to know that he wasn't getting any more rest than she was, lying in a lonely bed, wondering what had possessed her to fall in love with a man who was incapable of returning that love.

The thought of his rejection tore at her heart like a rusty knife. Blinking back the traitorous tears stinging her lids, she reached into her bag. "Damn, damn, damn."

"What's wrong?" Stephan asked, instantly concerned.

"I'm out of candy."

He threw back his head and laughed. "Is that all?"

Chantal glanced over at Caine, thinking how he'd taken to carrying the snacks in his pockets. Perhaps he had some now. But her pride was a hard, fierce thing; she'd die before ever asking him for anything again.

"It's not funny," she complained.

"Of course it's not." A small smile tugged at the corners of his lips. "So why don't we leave and go to a supermarket? I'll buy you a jumbo-size bag."

"I can't leave without Caine's permission."

He clucked his tongue, eyeing her with renewed interest. "This is definitely not the Chantal Giraudeau I've always known and loved. The young, devil-may-care princess who drove her family to distraction on more than one occasion. It's obvious that this O'Bannion fellow has domesticated you, love."

"That's ridiculous. I'm the same as ever."

"Are you?"

No, she could have answered, she wasn't the same at all. She'd had her heart broken into a thousand pieces, and there had been times during the past forty-eight hours that she wasn't really certain she wanted to keep on living.

"Of course."

"Prove it by ditching that Saint Bernard over there. The way you managed to shake your governess that New Year's Eve so many years ago."

She'd been fifteen, madly in love with twenty-year-old Stephan, or so she'd thought at the time, and desperate to see the New Year in with him. Unfortunately, her parents, as well as her governess, had other ideas, but Chantal had managed to get around their objections by climbing down the tree whose branches overhung her bedroom balcony.

The dare lay there between them, waiting for her to pick it up. "All right," she agreed, tilting her chin with renewed determination.

Stephan was right; she'd allowed Caine to domesticate her, to turn her into a weak, lovesick shadow of her former self. She was a survivor, she reminded herself now. A princess. Who was he to tell her what to do, where to go and with whom?

"I'll meet you out by the parking lot in five minutes."

"That's my girl." He bent his head and pressed his smiling lips against hers. "Five minutes."

Jealousy clawing at his insides, Caine caught her arm as she walked by him on the way back into the museum alone. "Where are you going?"

She jerked free of his hold. "None of your business."

"Now there's where you're wrong. Because in case you've forgotten, Princess, you just happen to be my business."

Her temper flared. "How could I forget when you keep throwing it up in my face? And now that you've brought it up yet again, I believe this is where I tell you that I'm sick and tired of being an assignment to an ill-tempered, cold-hearted man who is afraid to get close to anyone. And who is afraid to let anyone get close to him."

The words hurt more than he would have thought possible. "Tough."

There was no getting through to him. She'd tried everything she knew, even permitting Stephan to kiss her. She couldn't believe that Caine didn't love her; she'd seen it in his eyes too many times, felt it in his tender touch. But he steadfastly continued to deny his feelings, perhaps even to himself.

Taking a deep breath, Chantal looked up at him, her resolutely dry eyes hardened to a metallic sheen. "I thought you were a hero, Caine. But I was wrong. You're a coward."

This time when she pulled away from him, Caine didn't stop her. Instead, he simply followed her through the throng of people to the private ladies' lounge, where he stood guard outside the door, ignoring the interested glances from the women entering and exiting. It appeared she was going to sulk for quite some time, he determined, after she'd been in the room for several minutes. That was okay with him; he was prepared to wait all night.

Chantal had seen the window earlier. Now, upon closer examination, she realized it was a good deal higher and several inches narrower than she remembered. After waiting for the room to empty, she dragged a velvet-covered stool from the vanity to stand on. When her high heels made her footing too treacherous, she kicked them off, but without the added height, she had to jump several times before getting hold of the windowsill. She pulled herself up and through the narrow opening.

Success! She landed on the grass in her stocking feet. Then, ignoring the curious glances of passersby, she hurried to the parking lot, where she found Stephan waiting for her.

"Caine is very intelligent," she warned, glancing nervously over her shoulder. "I don't think we have much time."

"I've got the car right here," he said, putting his arm around her waist and leading her to a sleek black Ferrari. The car's engine was running loudly, sounding as if it would much prefer to be operating at top speed instead of idling here, waiting for its owner.

"Let's go, *chérie*," he said, opening the door for her. "It's high time you found out exactly how much fun the City of Angels can be."

As he drove off with a roar of the engine, Chantal experienced an unexpected stab of guilt at playing such a dirty trick on Caine. But he deserved it, she reminded herself. And besides, it wasn't as if she had run off with a stranger. She'd known Stephan all her life. He was family.

After five minutes had passed and there was no sign of Chantal, Caine decided the time had come to have this out. Marching into the gilt and mirrored lounge, he cursed when he found it deserted. The only thing left of the princess was a pair of ridiculously high-heeled Italian shoes.

"WHERE ARE WE GOING?" Chantal asked as she bit off a piece from her chocolate bar. They'd stopped at a convenience market down the coast road from the Malibu museum.

"I thought I'd show you my house. It's just up the coast."

"Oh, you live on the ocean? How wonderful," Chantal said, leaning back in the seat and enjoying the feel of the wind whipping her hair through the car's sunroof. Coming from a landlocked country, she'd always found the sea especially exhilarating. "I envy you."

He shrugged as he pulled off the road and headed down a long, curving road. "It's just a house. Nothing like what you're used to." They stopped in front of a set of blazing white walls. Stephan pressed a code into his car's security console, and the gates opened, permitting entrance. A few hundred yards down the curving roadway, another gate appeared.

"You certainly have a great deal of security," she said, thinking that even her father's palace wasn't so elaborately guarded.

"All the better to protect gorgeous princesses who might drop by for a visit," he said with a grin that had once possessed the power to melt her heart. At the moment it only served as an uncomfortable reminder of how she'd let Stephan goad her into pulling a dirty trick on a man who, personal feelings aside, had only wanted to protect her.

"Perhaps I should return to the museum," she said. "Caine will be worried."

"If you're truly concerned, it'd be faster to call him from the house. We're almost there."

They tore around one last turn before pulling up a curving flagstone driveway, stopping in front of a six-car garage. Chantal stared, entranced.

Viewing the stone, old-world manor house, situated in a dreamlike setting among cypress and pine trees and a eucalyptus grove, was like going back in time to the elegance and grace of the turn of the century. There were chimneys everywhere and formal gardens with flowing fountains. Giant marble sculptures flanked the massive front doors.

"It's not at all the home I would have expected you to own," she said as she entered the two-story, Italian-tiled entry.

"Oh? And what were you expecting?"

She shrugged as her wondering eyes took in the museum-quality sixteenth-century tapestry chair, the Sevres cachepots that held superb arrangements of freshly cut hothouse flowers, and a large, gilt-framed painting she recognized as Picasso's *Harlequin with a Glass*.

"I don't know. Something sleek and modern. All red-wood and windows, I suppose," she murmured. "But this . . ." Her voice drifted off as she tried to recall what Stephan's house reminded her of. "Why, it reminds me of the palace on Lake Losange," she said as recognition dawned.

"That's very clever of you, Chantal," Stephan said, leading her into a vast formal salon. The enormous crystal chandelier sent sparkling rainbows winking over the Empire furniture and silk-draped walls covered with priceless paintings. A pair of fencing foils hung on one wall, their hilts adorned with precious jewels. "I had the architect design a facsimile of the palace, although unfortunately, with California property values being what they are, I was forced to decrease the scale."

His hand rested lightly on her back, and he was smiling down at her. Yet there was an edge to his voice she had never heard before. A hint of restrained anger that caused a frisson of fear to skim up her spine.

"I think I'd better call Caine now."

"Why don't we have a drink first." He walked over to where a bottle of champagne was chilling in a silver bucket.

"I'd rather call Caine." The sickly sweet smell of lilies in a Tiffany Favrile glass vase was beginning to make her head ache.

There was a slight pop as he pulled the cork from the bottle. As she watched, he poured the golden effervescent wine into a pair of thin-stemmed, tulip-shaped glasses.

"I'm afraid that's impossible, *ma chère*," he said, holding one of the glasses toward her.

She heard a sound behind her and whipped around, hoping against hope that it was Caine; that she hadn't outsmarted him, after all. That he'd come to rescue her once again. When she came face-to-face with the bearded blond man she remembered all too well from Philadelphia, her blood turned cold.

"You," she whispered.

Reaching out with a gloved hand, the man traced her lips with his thumb. "So, Princess," he murmured, trailing his treacherous hand slowly down her throat, "we meet again."

# 14

"YOU LOOK a tad nervous, *ma chère*," Stephan said politely. "Are we making you uncomfortable?"

Chantal swallowed, knowing that the horrible man could feel her fear under his fingertips. "What do you think?"

He shook his head. "And here I'd always thought of myself as a superb host. Speaking of manners, may I introduce my good friend, Karl. After his little failure in Philadelphia, he's been looking forward to meeting you again. Haven't you Karl?"

"Yeah."

The man's cold blue eyes gleamed as he intimately regarded her body; his blatant perusal made her flesh crawl. His narrow face still bore the angry red scratches inflicted by her fingernails when she had struggled to fight him off.

"I don't understand," Chantal protested. "Why are you doing this, Stephan?"

He smiled at her over the rim of his champagne glass, but his eyes held no warmth. "You are an intelligent woman, Chantal. Surely you can figure it out."

"You're the one behind all my accidents?"

"I can't claim credit for them all," Stephan said. "Only the fire." He shook his head. "Personally, I felt that was the most ingenious plan of all. It would have succeeded, too, had it not been for your lover."

A violence she never would have suspected was in Stephan seemed very close to the surface. Chantal tried to concentrate on what Drew had said about Caine. His dedication to duty, his professionalism. His unwillingness to fail at any assigned task. *Oh, please, Caine*, she thought as she struggled to get hold of her whirling thoughts, *please come. Quickly.*

"What makes you think Caine is my lover?" she asked, stalling for time.

"What do you take us for, Chantal? Fools? It is obvious to anyone with eyes that O'Bannion has been sleeping with you from the beginning. Karl has become quite jealous, in fact. Haven't you, Karl?"

As his fingers trailed slowly across her shoulder blades, the blond man uttered a guttural grunt Chantal took to be an affirmative response.

"I'm quite fond of Karl," Stephan confirmed conversationally. "Despite the fact that he has one unpleasant little quirk."

"'Quirk'?"

"Idiosyncrasy," he translated the unfamiliar word. "He enjoys inflicting pain upon women."

Chantal found the implacable cruelty in Stephan's eyes every bit as disturbing as Karl's alleged perversity. "Why do you want to hurt me, Stephan?" she asked quietly. "What have I ever done to you?"

"What have you done? Why, nothing, *chérie*."

"I don't understand." She backed away from the silent Karl, relieved when he remained where he was, watching her with unblinking reptilian eyes.

Stephan reached into a desk drawer and pulled out a pack of long, dark brown cigarettes. "You know that my Aunt Clea died six months ago," he said as he lit one of the cigarettes with a thin gold lighter.

Burke's mother. "Of course. Although I'd never met her, I was sorry to hear she'd died. At the time, the news seemed to hit Burke very hard."

"She committed suicide. Hung herself with her bed sheets."

"How horrible!" Chantal wondered fleetingly if her brother had been told the truth and decided that he hadn't. She and Burke shared everything; he would not have kept such disturbing news to himself.

Stephan exhaled slowly, eyeing her through a veil of thick blue smoke. "Her father was the one who discovered her, during his monthly visit to the sanitorium. Did you know that he never stopped visiting her? For thirty-five years he made that unhappy trek from Montacroix to Switzerland in order to visit the beloved daughter your father had locked away so he would be free to marry his American slut."

"That's not the way it happened," she protested. "Clea was mentally ill. She'd been in the sanitorium for nearly five years when Papa met my mother."

"She was unhappy," he corrected. "And who wouldn't be? Living with a man who continually degraded her by sleeping with other women. By bringing his filthy whores into the palace."

"My father did no such thing!"

"Of course he did. Which is why my aunt had no choice but to end his worthless life."

"She tried to kill him?"

"He deserved it. Unfortunately, she failed and as a result was locked away so the truth could never get out."

"She was insane," Chantal repeated firmly.

"She was wronged!" Stephan roared, jabbing the cigarette into a crystal ashtray. Reaching into the drawer again, he pulled out a pistol and pointed it at her. "Eduard Gi-

raudeau made my aunt suffer for years. He has made her
family suffer. He is responsible for the death of an innocent, lovely woman. And now Clea's grieving father wants
the bastard Giraudeau to know exactly how it feels to lose
a daughter."

She remembered her father telling her that Clea's own
mother had committed suicide in a mental institution, that
insanity ran in the family. A fact that was all too apparent
as Stephan approached her, undisguised malice glittering
in his eyes.

"How can you talk this way? We have always been such
good friends, Stephan." She put her hand out, schooling
her voice to a calm, reassuring tone. "More than friends.
When I was a young girl, I loved you madly." Perhaps
"madly" wasn't the proper word, under the circumstance, she decided. "Wildly."

He shook his head. "You say you love me. But you sleep
with O'Bannion."

*Stall,* her fevered mind cried out, seizing the slim thread
of opportunity. "I didn't realize that you still cared for me."
Taking a chance, she reached over to put a supplicating
hand on his arm. "Had I known you wanted me, Stephan,
I never would have wasted my time with Caine."

She'd no sooner said his name when, as if conjured out
of thin air by wishful thinking, Chantal caught a glimpse
of Caine standing in the shadows of the foyer. He'd come.
As she'd known all along he would.

"Dear, dear Stephan," she murmured, her voice half
honey, half smoke, "don't you know that a woman never
forgets her first love?" She was grateful for her youthful
acting experience as she watched Stephan's eyes momentarily glaze over. He was obviously not immune to her
gently stroking fingers. "Please, darling. Send Karl away
so that we can be alone, just the two of us."

The spell snapped as quickly as it had been spun. "You're attempting to take my mind off what I must do," Stephan said. Although his eyes had cleared somewhat, Chantal could still see the madness glittering in their swirling depths. "You are no better than your mother, using your body to gain favors."

"That's not what I was doing," she protested.

"Of course it was. And it will not work. But don't worry, Princess," he said, caressing her cheek with the cold blue steel muzzle of the gun. "Karl and I will make certain that your last few hours are enjoyable."

The idea of either man touching Chantal made Caine's mind explode with fury. He wanted to kill them both, here and now, but unfortunately, Chantal was in the way. As if she'd read his mind, Chantal suddenly appeared to faint, folding bonelessly to the floor.

"What the hell?" Stephan burst out.

As the two men bent over her, Caine rushed into the room, bringing his revolver down toward the base of Stephan's skull. It might have been instinct, or perhaps he'd felt the faint whoosh of air, but Stephan ducked and rolled out of the way. Caine's blow connected with his shoulder, however, and the force dislodged the pistol, sending it skittering across the black marble flooring.

As Stephan reached for the gun, Chantal came alive. Jumping up and grabbing the gilded foil from the wall, she pointed it toward him. "Don't you dare move, Stephan," she warned softly, "or I'll kill you."

Not to be left out, Karl had pulled his own snub-nosed revolver and was pointing it at Caine.

"It appears that we have ourselves a standoff, O'Bannion," Stephan observed. "Even if you do manage to shoot Karl before he gets you, I'll still have Chantal."

"Brave words from an unarmed man," Caine said, watching both men carefully.

"You forget, I know Chantal. You wouldn't hurt a fly, would you, *ma chère*?" He glanced over at his pistol, just out of reach. "We have a treat for you, O'Bannion. You're going to get to watch your slut perform first with me and then with Karl. And when we're through with her, she's going to watch you die."

As he grabbed for his weapon, Chantal lunged, plunging the sharp tip of the foil into the back of his hand. At the unexpected pain, Stephan screamed, distracting Karl just long enough for Caine to kick the gun out of his hand.

Then Caine fell on the blond man and began using his hands with startling efficiency. This was the man who'd tried to kill Chantal. The man who'd left her in that smoked-filled house to die. Blind with rage, he drove his fists into the man's face again and again until he lay unconscious.

"Caine! Caine! Please stop. You're going to kill him!"

Through the roaring in his ears, he heard Chantal's frantic voice. Shaking his head as if to clear it, he turned around. She was standing there, her foil pressed against Stephan's chest, her eyes wide with fright.

"You want to be next?" he asked Stephan, picking up both guns from the floor as he walked over to where the man lay.

"You may think you've won, O'Bannion, but you haven't. Fate has decreed that I kill the bastard princess, and I will not fail."

"Don't look now, pal, but your plan's gone down the drain," Caine said, uncurling Chantal's rigid fingers from the foil.

"Destiny will not be denied!" Stephan shouted. "The princess must die in retaliation for Princess Clea's death."

"He really is insane," she said faintly as Stephan let loose with a long, incoherent tirade against her family.

"Mad as a hatter."

"Drew was right." Her smile, as she looked up at him, only wobbled slightly. "You are a hero. You saved my life."

He brushed his fingertips down her cheek. "Then we're even. Because you saved mine."

The reluctant love he felt for her was so apparent in his eyes that Chantal had to bite her lip to keep from crying out his name. "Caine," she uttered simply.

It was only his name, but her tone spoke volumes. Before he could respond, Drew walked in the door, two FBI men right behind him.

"Nice of you to drop by," Caine said.

"Hey, you said you wanted first dibs on the guy," Drew said with a broad grin. "I figured you'd have everything under control by now." He put away his gun. "So your hunch about the cousin proved right, after all."

Chantal stared at him. "You knew about Stephan? How?"

Caine shrugged. "All this seemed so personal, I started wondering if your would-be assassin's grudge might be against your father rather than you. Remembering what you said about his first wife's insanity, I called the institution where she'd been hospitalized and discovered that she had committed suicide shortly before the first attempt on your life."

"Since that pointed toward a motive for revenge, we ran a check on all the family members and discovered that not only had Clea's nephew, one Stephan Devouassoux, recently visited Montacroix, but his credit card revealed that he was also in Washington, New York and Philadelphia on the same days as your exhibit," Drew tacked on.

"Figuring he'd try again, we asked Burke to tell him where you were, if he happened to ask," Caine continued, "which he did. But since we didn't have any hard proof that he was behind your rash of accidents, and simply wanting to know your whereabouts wasn't any crime, we've had the guy under surveillance ever since his call to you in Milwaukee."

"But you didn't say a word," Chantal said.

"I was going to, as soon as we got to L.A. But the way things were going between us, I didn't think you'd believe me."

Chantal looked down at the two men on the floor, one rubbing his battered face as he groggily regained consciousness, the other glaring up at her with an icy malevolence that chilled her blood. "I probably wouldn't have. It's so unbelievable. Stephan and I were always so close." She shook her head.

Displaying the tenderness that had been missing from their relationship during the past two days, Caine put his arm around Chantal's waist. "Ready to go back to the hotel?"

She was in no mood to argue. "Ready." Leaning against him, she allowed him to shepherd her to the car.

THE FOLLOWING DAY, Chantal was alone in her hotel suite, packing to return to Montacroix, when there was a knock on her door. Opening it, her heart soared when she viewed Caine standing there. She hadn't seen him since the FBI and the Los Angeles police had questioned her last night.

"Hi," she said, feeling unreasonably shy.

Caine looked no more comfortable. "Hi. I came to see if you're ready for your bags to be taken downstairs."

"The bellman could have done that."

"As you so succinctly pointed out three weeks ago, it's my job to carry all those bags. I like to see a job through to the end."

She forced a smile. "I'm almost finished. Would you like to come in and wait?"

"Sure." Clothes were piled high on the bed, colorful, expensive silks and satins, most of which he recognized. "I got a call from Montacroix this morning."

Chantal looked up from her renewed packing. He was standing in the bedroom doorway, military straight as always, his expression unreadable. "Oh?"

"Clea's father has been arrested for plotting your murder. Since there's no sign of mental instability, it doesn't look as if he's going to be able to use Stephan's insanity defense, so I suspect he'll probably be put away for a very long time."

She shook her head as she picked up a peach-colored satin teddy that unstopped a flood of memories Caine had been struggling to forget. "Poor man."

Caine fought the urge to go to her. "That poor man tried to kill you, Chantal."

"I know." Tucking the teddy into a corner of the suitcase, she began folding the ivory nightgown she'd been wearing the first time he'd made love to her.

Desire slammed into Caine. He unrelentingly forced it down.

"But it's such a tragedy, Caine. So many years. So many lives."

"I talked with your father. He's relieved. But I think he's feeling a bit guilty about everything, too."

"Papa has this unfortunate tendency to believe that he can control the entire world around him," Chantal observed. *Like someone else I know,* she could have tacked on. "Whenever things go awry in his carefully constructed utopia, he believes it to be his fault."

When Caine didn't answer, Chantal fell silent, as well. "Well," she said at length, "I guess that's everything."

He'd never wanted a woman more than he wanted Chantal. Never needed a woman more than he needed her. "So, looks as if you're all set."

"I suppose so."

As Caine struggled to keep his expression from revealing his inner turmoil, he marveled at Chantal's ability to conceal her own thoughts so well. Her too-pale face was disconcertingly void of expression.

"I'm supposed to be downtown at police headquarters for a debriefing in thirty minutes, so Drew was scheduled to drive you to the airport," he said. "But I don't think Lieutenant Martin would mind if I changed our appointment to later this afternoon."

Chantal stared up at him, wondering if this was Caine's way of telling her that he'd changed his mind. But then she read the terrible finality in his eyes and realized that all he was offering was companionship to the airport.

"Drew's been doing all the driving up until now," she said. "He may as well continue."

Caine shrugged. "Whatever you want."

It was a statement Chantal didn't dare answer. She refused to give the man the satisfaction of knowing that her heart was breaking. Instead, she walked from the room, leaving Caine to follow with the bags.

They stood close together on the sidewalk in front of the hotel. "Chantal—"

"Yes?" Hope leaped into her eyes, only to fade away as she took in Caine's shuttered gaze.

"Take care."

"You, too," she managed through lips that had turned to stone. "And thank you. For everything." She turned away, then, unable to leave without one last bittersweet memory, she lifted her hand to his cheek. "You know, Caine," she said softly, "no one expects you to be bullet-proof." Going up on her toes, she pressed her lips against his, igniting a quick flare of heat that was too soon gone.

Climbing into the front seat of the limousine, she quickly closed the door, continuing to stare straight ahead out the windshield until Drew had driven the car around the corner. Then she buried her face in her hands and wept.

After a time her sobs diminished, and Chantal drew in a deep, painful breath as she accepted the clean white handkerchief Drew extended across the center console.

"Thought you might need this," he said simply.

As she wiped her eyes, Chantal couldn't help wondering why she hadn't been smart enough to fall in love with a simple, uncomplicated man. A man like Drew Tremayne, for instance.

"You're going to make some woman a wonderful husband."

He grinned. "That's what my mama always says, right after she asks me how come I'm still not married."

"And what do you tell her?"

"That if I ever find the right woman, I'll move heaven and earth to get her."

And he would, too, Chantal knew. Drew was the kind of man who'd put his head down and forge full steam ahead. Depending on the woman he chose, such a damn-the-torpedoes, single-minded pursuit could either prove exhilarating or frightening.

"I love him, Drew."

"I know, honey. And I think you're a smart enough cookie to realize that he loves you, too."

"So where does that leave us?"

He reached over and took her hand in his. "Give him some time, Chantal. Caine's not as dumb as he looks. He's bound to realize that he can't live without a certain princess in his life." He shot her an encouraging grin. "In the meantime, there's a little going away present for you in the glove compartment."

Leaning forward, Chantal investigated, laughing in spite of her pain when she discovered the cache of chocolate-covered peanuts.

TWO NIGHTS LATER, Caine and Drew sat in a dimly lit neighborhood bar where the jazz was cool and the drinks weren't watered. "I always knew you were an idiot," Drew said, popping a handful of beer nuts into his mouth. "But I never realized you were certifiably crazy."

Caine lifted the bottle of dark beer to his mouth and took a long pull. "Now you're talking about Chantal."

"Who else? Do you have any idea how many men would commit murder to be in your shoes? She loves you, Caine."

"And I love her. But it's not enough."

"So you keep saying." Drew leaned back in his chair and took another handful of nuts. "You know, women have an unfortunate tendency not to wait around forever. Even for a man they love." Calm brown eyes observed Caine soberly. "Go to her, Caine. Before you spend the rest of your life wishing you had."

Drew wasn't saying anything that Caine hadn't been telling himself over and over again since he'd watched Chantal drive out of his life. "I'll think about it," he muttered, ignoring his friend's triumphant expression.

IT WAS A WARM spring evening, that special time between afternoon and night when the world seems to stop and catch its breath. The sun was a brilliant orange ball dipping into Lake Losange, turning the cloudless sky to jeweled tones of ruby, amethyst and gold. A light breeze rippled the sun-gilded water.

She was sitting on a rock, looking out over the lake, clad in a snug tank top and white shorts that displayed her long legs to advantage. It had been two weeks. Fourteen long and incredibly lonely days and even lonelier nights.

"Looks like good sailing weather."

At the sound of Caine's voice, Chantal closed her eyes briefly, then turned around. Noel's dream, predicting it would happen exactly this way, had been the only thing that kept her from going to Caine in Washington. She'd wanted to believe her sister; she'd clung to the happy premonition the way a seven-year-old clings to thoughts of Saint Nicholas. But deep in her heart she'd been afraid that it was only wishful thinking.

"Hello, Caine," she said with studied calm, wondering if he could see the galloping beat of her heart. "Whatever are you doing here?"

Her haughty tone was pure princess, but in her eyes he caught a glimpse of the Chantal he'd come to love. "I don't suppose you'd believe I came to bring you these." Reaching into his suit-jacket pocket, he pulled out a handful of silver-wrapped chocolate kisses.

She longed to go to him, but pride kept her where she was. "Since Switzerland is just across the border and world famous for its chocolate, I feel obliged to point out that it's a bit like carrying coals to Newcastle."

She wasn't going to make it easy on him. Caine wondered why he'd thought she might.

"I lied." He dropped the candies back into his pocket.

"Oh?"

"I didn't come all this way to bring you any damned candy."

"I didn't think you had." Something else occurred to her. "How did you find me out here?"

"Burke gave me a ride from the airport. Noel said you liked to walk along the lake this time of day."

"It sounds as if my family's orchestrating my life again."

"They love you.... I love you." He was amazed at how good those three simple words made him feel. Why had it taken him so damn long to say them?

"I know."

She was too calm. Too remote. He walked over to her, his stomach twisting into knots as he took both her hands in his and drew her to her feet. "And you love me," he insisted.

"I did." She took a deep breath, trying to turn away, but Caine wouldn't let her. "I don't any longer."

"And I thought *I* was a rotten liar."

"Even if I did love you," she said reluctantly, "and I'm not saying I do, what difference would it make? Someone once told me that love wasn't always enough." The hardness in her eyes was softening slowly, hesitantly. But it was a beginning.

"I've always thought you were an intelligent woman."

"I thought I was, too." *Until I let my heart run away with my head,* she could have added, but didn't.

"So why would such an intelligent woman pay any attention to an idiot jerk who didn't know what he was talking about?" The evening breeze ruffled her hair; Caine brushed it away from her face with hands so remarkably gentle that Chantal's breath caught in her throat.

"If I remember correctly, you were against marriage because of your career. It was too dangerous, you said. Have you changed your mind in a mere two weeks?"

"I may have been wrong about that," he admitted. "But it's a moot point. I've resigned from Presidential Security."

"But why?"

Caine shrugged. "Several reasons. One of them being all the guns I've had pointed at me in the past three months. I'm getting too old for that cops and robbers stuff."

"What will you do?"

"Drew and I are setting up a private security firm. Nothing dangerous, just surveillance—sweeping offices for electronic eavesdropping devices, that sort of thing." As nervous as he was, Caine managed a smile. "Fortunately, everyone in Washington is so paranoid about bugs, we've already got more jobs than we can handle."

"I'm pleased for you."

"Thanks."

Silence settled over them. "Why did you come here, Caine?" she asked finally, looking up at him, her eyes wide and vulnerable.

She'd already been hurt more than any one person deserved. Caine vowed that he'd never allow anything, or anyone—himself included—to hurt Chantal ever again.

"To ask you to marry me." He took a deep breath. "I love you, Chantal. And I want to have a family with you. Kids, dogs, a station wagon, the whole works."

"The big, sprawling house in the country," she said softly, remembering their conversation.

"With the wide front porch for watching our neighbors. Rose bushes in the front yard and a big tree in the back for a swing. And something I forgot to mention—a studio, with lots of high, wide windows and skylights for the family's resident artist." He framed her uplifted face in

palms. "No one has ever made me want those things.
woman until you."

A shimmering golden joy coursed through her. "There's
mething you need to know, Caine, before I give you my
swer."

"What's that?"

"We are a little old-fashioned here in Montacroix. Al-
ough I realize that the rest of the world might consider
an anachronism, it is traditional to ask the father for his
ughter's hand."

It was going to be all right. They were going to be all
ht. "I know. Burke warned me before I arrived."

"And?"

"And your father insists on the wedding being held in
e palace chapel before I take you home with me to
ashington. Your mother, as we speak, is planning the
ception menu with the kitchen staff, Noel has been put
charge of floral arrangements and musicians, and Burke
on his way into town to bribe the parish priest into for-
ing the usual four-week posting of the banns."

"My brother would never bribe anyone, let alone a
iest."

"Correction, my mistake. It's not a bribe. It's a dona-
n to the church building fund."

"My, my," she murmured. "Everyone certainly sounds
a hurry to get me married off."

Caine grinned, that rare, wonderful smile that Chantal
ew would still have the power to thrill her when she was
nety.

"I think they're all anxious for me to make an honest
oman of you," he said, lowering his lips to hers. Cup-
ng the back of her neck, he lingered over the kiss. "So
hat's your answer, Princess? Are you going to make your

family—and the man who loves you—very, very happy, or not?"

"I'll marry you, Caine, on one condition."

Caine didn't hesitate. "Name it."

As she twined her arms around his neck, the brightness of Chantal's smile rivaled the dazzling Montacroix sunset. "I won't darn your socks."

# HARLEQUIN Temptation

# COMING NEXT MONTH

In April, Harlequin brings you the
world's most popular romance author

# JANET DAILEY

## *No Quarter Asked*

### Out of print since 1974!

After the tragic death of her father, Stacy's world is shattered. She
needs to get away by herself to sort things out. She leaves behind
her boyfriend, Carter Price, who wants to marry her. However, as
soon as she arrives at her rented cabin in Texas, Cord Harris, owner
of a large ranch, seems determined to get her to leave. When Stacy
has a fall and is injured, Cord reluctantly takes her to his own ranch.
Unknown to Stacy, Carter's father has written to Cord and asked
him to keep an eye on Stacy and try to convince her to return home.
After a few weeks there, in spite of Cord's hateful treatment that
involves her working as a ranch hand and the return of Lydia, his ex-
fiancée, by the time Carter comes to escort her back, Stacy knows
that she is in love with Cord and doesn't want to go.

### Watch for *Fiesta San Antonio* in July and
*For Bitter or Worse* in September.

## HARLEQUIN
### American Romance®

Live the

Rocky Mountain Magic

Become a part of the magical events at The Stanley Hotel in the Colorado Rockies, and be sure to catch its final act in April 1990 with #337 RETURN TO SUMMER by Emma Merritt.

Three women friends touched by magic find love in a very special way, the way of enchantment. Hayley Austin was gifted with a magic apple that gave her three wishes in BEST WISHES (#329). Nicki Chandler was visited by psychic visions in SIGHT UNSEEN (#333). Now travel into the past with Kate Douglas as she meets her soul mate in RETURN TO SUMMER #337.

ROCKY MOUNTAIN MAGIC—All it takes is an open heart.

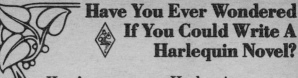

# Have You Ever Wondered If You Could Write A Harlequin Novel?

Here's great news—Harlequin is offering a series of cassette tapes to help you do just that. Written by Harlequin editors, these tapes give practical advice on how to make your characters—and your story—come alive. There's a tape for each contemporary romance series Harlequin publishes.

**Mail order only**

**All sales final**

---

# The Adventurer

## JAYNE ANN KRENTZ

Remember THE PIRATE (Temptation #287), the first book of Jayne Ann Krentz's exciting trilogy Ladies and Legends? Next month Jayne brings us another powerful romance, THE ADVENTURER (Temptation #293), in which Kate, Sarah and Margaret — three long-time friends featured in THE PIRATE — meet again.

A contemporary version of a great romantic myth, THE ADVENTURER tells of Sarah Fleetwood's search for long-lost treasure and for love. Only when she meets her modern-day knight-errant Gideon Trace will Sarah know she's found the path to fortune and eternal bliss....

THE ADVENTURER — available in April 1990! And in June look for THE COWBOY (Temptation #302), the third book of this enthralling trilogy.